"First." She put up a finger. "I am not squatting. I signed a contract with your—Madame Desauliers.

"Second. And this is off the topic, but strangely, very key," she iterated with a stab of her forefinger. "If you're married, then why the flirtation at the bakery this morning?"

About to spew a protest at her, Rez calmed his need to be right. It was work, and stress, and damn it, his struggles with Jean-Louis. This woman did not deserve his fury. Not until he found out what was actually going on.

"First," he said and put up a finger as well. "It's not a bakery. It is a patisserie."

The way her eyebrow arched in challenge teased him to smile, but Rez snatched back his waning righteousness.

"And second," he resumed, "I am no longer married."

Dear Reader,

I have written for many Harlequin series, including Luna, Bombshell, Nocturne and Intrigue. This is my first book in the Harlequin Romance series. So to begin with this new-to-me series, I wanted to work with elements that were comfortable to me. Paris is a favorite setting of mine. I've had the incredible opportunity to visit three times. Also, I wanted to write a heroine closer to my age. We don't stop daydreaming, crushing and romancing after a significant birthday. As well, my heroine is a widow, and I do, unfortunately, have experience with that.

As a writer, I often put a little piece of myself in every book. Be it a personality quirk, a favorite meal or hobby, or befriending a duck in Paris. There's a lot of me in this one. And I had fun bringing together the hero and heroine in a sweet but sexy affaire de coeur that will appeal to readers of any age. And you'd better believe that the next time I am in Paris, I will keep my eyes wide open for a sexy stranger buying opera cakes in a patisserie.

Michele

Cinderella's Second Chance in Paris

—

Michele Renae

HARLEQUIN®

Romance™

Recycling programs
for this product may
not exist in your area.

ISBN-13: 978-1-335-73694-9

Cinderella's Second Chance in Paris

Copyright © 2022 by Michele Hauf

All rights reserved. No part of this book may be used or reproduced in
any manner whatsoever without written permission except in the case of
brief quotations embodied in critical articles and reviews.

This is a work of fiction. Names, characters, places and incidents
are either the product of the author's imagination or are used fictitiously.
Any resemblance to actual persons, living or dead, businesses,
companies, events or locales is entirely coincidental.

For questions and comments about the quality of this book,
please contact us at CustomerService@Harlequin.com.

Harlequin Enterprises ULC
22 Adelaide St. West, 41st Floor
Toronto, Ontario M5H 4E3, Canada
www.Harlequin.com

Printed in U.S.A.

Michele Renae is the pseudonym for award-winning author Michele Hauf. She has published over ninety novels in historical, paranormal and contemporary romance and fantasy, as well as action/adventure under the name Alex Archer. Instead of "writing what she knows," she prefers to write "what she would love to know and do" (and yes, that includes being a jewel thief and/or a brain surgeon).

You can email Michele at toastfaery@gmail.com.
Instagram: @MicheleHauf
Pinterest: @ToastFaery

Cinderella's Second Chance in Paris
is Michele Renae's debut title for Harlequin.

Visit the Author Profile page at Harlequin.com.

This story is for anyone who has ever wondered if they can begin again. Yes. You can.

CHAPTER ONE

Paris

VIVIANE WESTBERG DIVIDED her attention between the luscious chocolate pastries behind the glass display counter and the equally snackable man standing to her right. He also perused the delightful offerings, for which any kid would shove aside their toys to eat on Christmas Morning.

A waft of spicy cologne teased Viv's nostrils more so than the sweets. The man oozed a subtle pheromone that demanded her attention. Tall, his figure was straight, clad in black trousers and a fitted white business shirt that jealously hugged his biceps and pecs. Diamond cufflinks flashed. He was clearly unafraid to flaunt his obvious wealth.

Dark stubble peppered his square jaw. Rich black hair, tousled but not messy, tickled the starched shirt collar. A few strands of silver woven into the black made her smile. Sexy and seasoned?

Rolling her eyes, and forcing her attention back on the pastries, Viv inwardly laughed at her thoughts. She had been in Paris three days and already she was eyeing up dating prospects?

Well. Diving back into the dating pool *was* on her shortlist. A woman could only survive so long without some companionship. And physical connection. That was on her list, along with kick-starting her new business. Exterior landscaping had been her gig the last two decades. Now she wanted to move it inside. Plans for her interior garden business had been on paper for a decade. And right now, in Paris, she planned to nurture that paper dream into a beautiful blossom.

As for dating? Her husband had passed away three years ago. She had loved Brian dearly. And yet this adventure across the ocean was all about Taking the Next Step. Yes, in capital letters. And, while she understood less than a percentage point of French, the melody of the language could seduce her into a swoon. If Monsieur Sexy of the diamond cufflinks acknowledged her with a glance, she might melt like the chocolate glaze gleaming in the morning sunlight.

Startled to realize the clerk behind the counter had prompted her for her order, Viv apologized— *pardon* was easy enough—and then pointed to the one Opera cake remaining on a mirrored platter. Coffee and buttercream? Yes, please!

Deploying her worst French, she said, *"Un, s'il vous plait."*

"Non, madame. Monsieur has already chosen that one." The clerk gestured to the sexy mystery man. "You select another."

"Oh, but I…"

As the pastry she'd wanted was drawn out and placed in a pink-and-cream-striped bag, Viv glanced to the man she had been drooling over. His broad shoulders rose in an apologetic shrug. Mercy, were his eyes really that blue? The corner of his mouth tilted up before blossoming into a full-on smile.

Viv's heart fluttered. Her neck heated.

"Sorry," he offered in English. "Might I suggest the *cerise gâteau*? It is a cherry cake. Delicious. You must try."

Oh, that voice. Deep and a little rough, as if he'd just woken. It brushed against her skin in a subtle tease. Promised kisses to swoon for. Anything he offered—she was up for.

Viv arrested her lusty thoughts before they swerved toward heavy breathing and bared body parts. "Cherry cake, then."

The clerk retrieved one of the small cakes.

The man turned to Viv and offered his hand to shake. "Rezin Ricard. I'm staying in the neighborhood for a few days and remembered how much I enjoy this shop's Opera cakes. You must be vacationing?"

Slipping her hand into his felt as if she'd entered a new realm. Was being led across a mysterious threshold into something bright and intriguing. He held her hand for a moment that felt like a lifetime. A sure, strong squeeze, and then he released her.

Feeling like a teenager who had been touched by her crush, Viv prayed her blush wouldn't flush her cheeks too brightly. Flustered, she made the save.

"I'm here for a few weeks," she offered. "For work, actually. I'm reviving an ill-cared-for indoor garden. It's down the street. I've been taking morning walks, and this bakery has become my reward for all those steps."

Oh, Viv! Too much information! Heck, she'd forgotten how small talk worked. It had been a long time since she'd engaged in such a thing with a man who was not her husband.

Body completely facing hers, and head slightly bowed to focus on her—as if she were the most important thing to him—he said, "Tell me what you've discovered about our city that surprised you."

"Oh…"

An intriguing question. And he seemed genuinely interested. Refreshing, especially after the cold shoulders she'd received from the locals and shop clerks who had to endure her ridiculous attempts at the language.

"The Tuileries is beautiful this early, with the dew on the ground. I think I made friends with a duck." Viv laughed nervously.

Really? A duck? Way to make a first impression with the stunningly sexy Frenchman.

"I do love the royal garden."

The man—Rezin—was prompted by the clerk. He spoke to her in rapid French that completely exceeded Viv's comprehension, then handed her a black credit card. Then he turned back to her. "If this is your morning routine, then perhaps I can hope to see you tomorrow around this time?"

Viv's jaw dropped open. Was he asking her for a date? No. It was just a polite comment. Maybe? That glint in his eyes certainly teased something. Was it, *I dare you*? Now she felt a flush of heat at her temples and trickling down the back of her neck.

Please let it be a pesky hot flash, and not a noticeable blush!

"I work on the Champs-Élysées," he added. "So I drive by here daily."

The Champs-Élysées was the famous elite street that featured luxury retailers that attracted celebrities and tourists in droves. However, Viv had counted a McDonalds and a few cell phone stores in the mix, even a Starbucks.

Rezin collected his credit card and the pastry bag, then winked at her. Winked!

"See you tomorrow," he said. "Uh…what is your name?"

"Viviane," she said on a breathy whisper.

"*Au revoir*, Viviane." He turned and walked out of the shop.

Mouth gaping again, Viv followed his strides until he was out of sight. A handsome Frenchman had suggested he wanted to see her again. Score! Maybe? Oh, heck, she'd take it.

When someone cleared their throat behind her, she had to force herself to turn around and resume normal Viv mode. As in your average American widow who had traveled to Paris to forge a new path in life. And, yes, to indulge in her fantasies about meeting a handsome Frenchman. Even though she knew they would remain fantasies. Because, really, she was not the sort of woman who could simply snag a French lover with a glance.

"Monsieur Ricard is very kind," the clerk said as she handed over Viv's bag to her. "No charge."

"What?" She shoved her hand in her back pocket, where she kept a ten-euro bill for snacks to fuel her morning explorations.

"Monsieur Ricard paid for yours. And…" the clerk gestured "…look inside."

Stunned and impressed at the man's generous move, Viv opened the bag. Inside sat the Opera cake.

"He asked me to do a swap." The clerk twirled her finger to emphasize the sneaky switch.

"Thanks," Viv said, and then corrected herself. *"Merci."*

Outside the shop, her smile exploded. She gripped the folded bag top with both hands. Precious cargo, gifted by a fantasy man. An inhalation lifted her chest as high as her spirits. That encounter would see her flying for the entire day.

And, since the rest of the day involved battling a nasty overgrowth of thorned and desiccated foliage, she would ride it for all it was worth.

The fifteen-minute stroll from Le Beau Boutique to the mansion nestled at the river's edge of the Eighth Arrondissement was a good way to shake the stress from his body.

Rezin Ricard had not called his driver to pick him up after work today. Because of the scarring on Rez's left leg, from the car accident, the muscles there tended to seize and make him limp. More so after a long day of sitting. To counter that, he found walking helped. He hadn't gone to physical therapy in over a year. No time.

He had been thankful this morning to walk away from a beautiful woman without showing signs of his limp. Sacrificing his favorite Opera cake for the sight of a pair of pretty green eyes? What an ego boost. And he did hope to see her tomorrow morning. If only to experience more of her difference. Viviane hadn't been like the locals, with their subtle yet precise style. Not like the tourists, with their souvenir tee shirts and gawking gazes. And not like…

Her.

Shoving aside a rise of memory that might lure him to brooding, Rez entered the digital code and walked through the narrow courtyard to his three-story eighteenth-century mansion. Pausing before the main doors, he tilted back his head to take in the June sunshine.

Work demanded he give a hundred and ten per cent—or risk losing it all. And lately, that extra ten per cent was trying him. He did need a break, but as owner and CEO of his jewelry business, Le Beau, he was not ready to retire. Nor could he conceive of his son, Jean-Louis, taking over and steering the company in the direction *he* desired—which involved celebrity endorsements and "focusing on the bling" as Jean-Louis put it.

Le Beau had been founded one hundred years ago, by Rez's great-grandfather. They designed and curated classic rare jewels and commissioned pieces. Glamorous, sumptuous, and elegant. In the worldwide realm of jewelers they were highly respected. And Rez had no intention of rebranding to focus on the bling.

Rez hadn't stood within these cool limestone and marble walls in years. For good reason. But his penthouse in the Sixth was being renovated. The herringbone wood floors were being refinished, the cabinets refaced, the wall between the kitchen and the living area he'd always wanted knocked out was finally coming down, and there would be many other refurbishments. And instead of staying at the Ritz, or Hotel Regina, he'd decided that this empty mansion would serve.

As well, it would give him time to let go of the memories of his wife that haunted him. This mansion had been Colette's folly…her *tanière*—her lair, as she'd called it. Much as she'd thrived in the spotlight—she'd modeled in her twenties and thirties—even she had needed to recharge on occasion.

Two black leather suitcases sat in the foyer. His driver, Henri, in possession of the entrance code, had delivered them hours earlier. The place was kept in order, with a monthly visit from a cleaning service. But food was not stocked. Easy enough to order in meals. He'd be fine here while he waited out the penthouse reconstruction.

As long as he didn't wander into the Victorian-style indoor greenhouse at the back of the mansion. There, Colette had fussed over her roses and her painting projects.

Following Colette's death two years ago, his mother-in-law, Coral, had insisted he keep this place. Rez had wanted to sell immediately. But Coral, a world traveler who did not intend to stop trotting across the globe until her bones ceased to move and her body simply gave up, used the mansion a few months out of the year, whenever her adventures returned her to France. As well, Jean-Louis had once mentioned he used it on occasion.

Marriage issues already? Rez didn't want to get involved. Not with the tenuous relationship he and his son currently held.

It was after eight p.m., and the light that he'd absorbed outside drifted through the kitchen windows to glimmer across the pristine marble countertops. Rez eyed the gleaming coffee maker. No. He wanted restful sleep tonight. Tomorrow promised a meeting with a new client, to design a wedding set for his fiancée. A prince of some Scandinavian country...

Rez couldn't remember the country's name. He hated it that little things slipped his mind. Since the accident, in which he'd suffered a concussion resulting in traumatic brain injury, his short-term memory played tricks with him.

A new name could slip his hold before the handshake had even separated. The fact that he'd pushed back his chair when standing would evaporate and he'd then sit down—to land on the floor. Add to that, the dizziness. He was getting better at anticipating when a dizzy spell would attack, and now he could prop his shoulder against a wall or grab the back of a chair to ride it out. Yet that physical malady was difficult to hide from his coworkers...and his son.

Tonight he wouldn't think about Jean-Louis's intentions to rebrand Le Beau. Not when his leg urged him to sit and relax. Some days he even used a cane. But that felt wrong. Thriving at fifty-five, he was fit, healthy, and shouldn't need to use a cane like a geriatric.

With a sigh, Rez opened the fridge. He was surprised to see bottles of water and juice, as well as fresh fruit and charcuterie. His driver must have left the provisions for him. Henri, who had been with the family two decades, was good to take care of him like that.

Grabbing a bottle of water, Rez glanced down the foyer toward the spiral staircase. He'd sleep in the second-floor guest room that faced the Eiffel Tower. Not the large bedroom that mastered the third floor and faced the Arc de Triomphe. *Their* bedroom.

He couldn't bring himself to even peek inside. He guessed that Coral must use it when she stayed, because she'd once mentioned that the size of the closet could fit all her worldly belongings. The mansion was huge—a Paris gem worth forty million. Should Rez list it, it would sell immediately.

And that was his intention.

But first he needed to say *au revoir.* It was the least he could do for the wife he had loved for thirty years. Even if he suspected she had not returned that love in the latter part of their marriage.

A crashing noise toward the back of the house alerted him. Rez limped down to the open foyer, beneath the massive crystal chandelier. Who was in the house? Had he hit on a day when the maid stopped in? Wasn't it a little late to be cleaning? Unless the crash had been someone breaking in? No, the exterior security system was top of the line.

Wincing at the pain in his leg, he neared the conservatory. The property was backed by a solid limestone wall, but it was easily climbable. Break one of the greenhouse windows, and—

Though the noise hadn't sounded like shattering glass.

The double doors to the conservatory were open and the inner light was on. Rez cautiously approached the room. Overgrown foliage frosted the windows and walls. Most of it was green, spots here and there wilting and brown. The two-story room looked like a jungle that defied tidying.

Calling out, he walked inside. "Who's in here?"

"What? Who's here?" a woman's voice called in English.

Green fronds jiggled to Rez's left, and out popped a blonde head. The woman was on her knees, which were stained with dirt, and she wielded a gardener's spade.

"It's okay. I bumped into the utility cart. I didn't know anyone else was here— Oh."

Her mouth dropped open.

Rez's anger softened from tight fists to utter confusion. It was the woman from the *pâtisserie*. He didn't understand why she was here, on her knees, looking as though she had a purpose and a reason to be in his home.

"*Madame*, you must explain yourself."

"Please." She held up a palm. "I don't understand French. Can you speak English?"

The audacity!

"You have no right," he said tightly in French. "This was her—"

He squeezed a fist near his thigh and coached his rising blood pressure into a simmer. Very well, if he wanted to get his point across he must use English.

"Get out. I don't know why you're here, but you must leave. Now."

Using the toppled cart to pull herself up to stand, the woman tugged down her dirt-smeared tee shirt and stomped her feet, which settled her rumpled pants. After a sweep of her hand over her messy ponytail, she propped her hands akimbo.

"Rezin Ricard, right?" she asked.

Untidy copper-blonde strands poked out around her hairline. She was a nymph emerged from a forest, little concerned that she'd been disturbed from her natural habitat.

"What are you doing in my home?" he insisted, unwilling to allow her tattered beauty to dissuade him from his righteous anger.

"I'm staying here. And it's not your home. It belongs to a woman. Coral… I don't recall her last name, but I have it in my phone…" She glanced toward an array of spilled gardening tools and piles of dead foliage.

"Coral Desauliers," Rez said. "She is my mother-in-law. She doesn't own this mansion."

"Oh? *Oh…*"

Her pale lips distracted Rez from his fury. Burnished rose, her mouth, and seemingly soft… Had she enjoyed the pastry as much as he'd enjoyed making sure it was hers?

"I'm sorry. Coral hired me to revive the garden. She said I could stay here while I work. A month, if needed, though I anticipate only two weeks. Mother-in-law? You're…married?"

A confused tilt of her head emphasized the streak of dirt on her cheek. Rez wanted to brush it away. Was her skin as soft and pale as it appeared? The nymph had been playing in the dirt…

But then he found his anger. "What does my marital status have to do with a stranger squatting in my home?"

Her mouth dropped open.

Really? She was getting angry at *him*? Everything about this situation put her in the wrong and him in the right. And he would not tolerate another woman treading his wife's *tanière*.

"First." She put up a finger. "I am not squatting. I signed a contract with Madame Desauliers. Second. And this is off the topic, but strangely very key," she iterated with a stab of her forefinger. "If you're married, then why the flirtation at the bakery this morning?"

About to spew a protest at her, Rez calmed his need to be right. It was work, and stress—and, damn it, his struggles with Jean-Louis. This woman did not deserve his fury. Not until he found out what was actually going on.

"First," he said, and put up a finger as well. "It's not a bakery. It is a *pâtisserie*."

The way her eyebrow arched in challenge teased him to smile, but Rez snatched back his waning righteousness.

"And second," he resumed, "I am no longer married."

It hurt to say it out loud. It had been two years. Removing his wedding band a year ago had been the hardest step he'd taken on this miserable journey called grief.

"Oh." Her shoulders dropped. She sighed. "Sorry. Divorce?"

He shook his head.

"Oh." She nodded. "I get it. I'm a widow, too."

He softened his stance at that confession.

"It's tough. Some days it's not so tough. Other days you think it can't get any worse." She pressed her lips together and lifted her shoulders. "Right. No need to state the obvious. Anyway, Monsieur, I'm sorry if you weren't informed about my working here, but I insist on staying. I don't have anywhere else to go. And I do have a contract with Coral. And— Well, what are you doing here? I wasn't told that anyone occupied the place. I've been here three days."

Three days she had been in his home? Touching his wife's precious garden?

He took in what once could have been called a garden. It hadn't been properly cared for since

Colette's death. The monthly cleaning service had made him aware they were not gardeners, but they did water occasionally. The room was in desperate need of care.

Rez's gaze landed on the overgrown rose bushes. They stretched almost as high as his chest but did not look healthy. No blossoms, and the leaves were curled and dry. Those had been Colette's pride and joy. No one must ever touch them.

"Monsieur?"

How strange that he'd met this woman that morning and had thrilled over their light banter. He'd even felt a boyish embarrassment should his limp be revealed to her. She was beautiful, and she'd seemed so normal, down-to-earth and welcoming, in the *pâtisserie*. A difference he'd wanted to embrace and hold and, he'd been looking forward to seeing her again.

Yet now that he did stand before her...

Rez cleared his throat. "This can't happen. Not now. I'm..." *Not prepared to allow another person to tread my wife's territory.* "I will call Coral and get this straightened out."

He turned to leave the room, but she rushed around him and blocked the open doorway.

"Please, I need this job," she said. "I used to be an exterior landscaper and then, when my husband died— Well. This is my pivot. I'm starting over. Designing and refurbishing indoor greenhouses is my new business. I'm calling it Glass

Houses. Or maybe The Plant Whisperer. Haven't decided which is more marketable yet. I've got a plan. It's all in my notebook."

She gestured to the mess of tools on the floor. An oversized red leatherbound journal lay amongst the scattered objects.

"This project is my maiden voyage. I can bring life back to this garden."

"Who said it needs life?" Rez hissed.

With that, he pushed around her and marched to the kitchen. He called Coral. The connection forwarded him to messages, where her recorded voice stated that she was on a cell-free sabbatical for the next four days.

Slamming the phone onto the counter, Rez hung his head. Was life not content to take away his wife, leave him mentally and physically scarred, and pit his only son against him? Now it had tossed a new twist into the mix. A beautiful woman with green eyes and a magnetic pull that demanded he not ignore her. A woman who intended to pull up the most precious memories he had of his wife.

CHAPTER TWO

UNSURE WHAT TO do after that unsettling exchange, Viv brushed the dirt from her chinos and tossed aside her gardening gloves. He couldn't kick her out. Well, he *could*, but she wouldn't allow it. This garden needed her help. And her future depended on her finishing the job so she could use it as an example to attract more clients. This was the testing ground for Glass Houses. Or The Plant Whisperer.

She really needed to decide on the name of her business. Harley Monroe, her assistant, who worked remotely from Minnesota and was currently "reviving her socials," had insisted she decide. And fast.

After showing her friend Kiara Kirk, a jet-setting international Realtor who sold luxury homes, her plans for an indoor garden rescue business, Kiara had been the one to hook her up with Coral and this home. Now here she was in Paris! Doing what she loved. And doing it well.

For over a decade she'd tried to convince her husband, Brian, to move indoors from exterior landscapes, but he had always refused. He'd been an outdoorsman, had loved the massive scale they'd worked with, and couldn't be bothered with some of the more delicate indoor work. Still, she'd never given up hope that someday her dreams of a more intimate, focused garden service would come to fruition. Using her experience with wholesalers, construction crews, botanists, spreadsheets, and even architectural design, she'd drawn up a detailed plan. And while she'd been dreaming, she'd included the European element. She'd always wanted to travel, to visit foreign gardens, to immerse herself in new worlds.

The couple of hundred thousand dollars she'd received from Brian's life insurance was enough to get her started. But from that she'd have to set something aside for living. Her social security benefits didn't kick in for another eight years.

Viv had started to believe that—with a lot of hard work—she had a future as an independent woman who could take care of herself.

Until Rezin had yelled at her, pummeling her confidence. He'd been so kind and charming in the bakery. For a few precious seconds he'd made her feel like a teenager swooning over a sexy guy.

Of course, if he hadn't known she was staying here then he had every right to be upset. Why had his mother-in-law offered Viv this job and the free stay if she didn't even own the place? While she'd not actually spoken to Coral, the woman had talked with Kiara, who had forwarded to Viv a one-page list of what was expected. Restore the garden, all expenses would be covered, and she could stay in a room at the mansion.

Yes, she'd signed an e-contract, but whether or not the contract was legal…

Viv knew she'd do whatever she could to stay. Sure, she could purchase a return flight and head back to the States. But what was there for her in small-town Minnesota? She had no intention of keeping a base for her business there. Harley worked from wherever she tended to roam. And Viv could to do the same.

Since her husband's death she'd taken up gig work—delivering groceries, dropping off fast food on people's doorsteps. A means to pay the bills and eat, since their landscape business had lost all its clients during that final year when they'd had to shut it down so she could care for Brian. The chemotherapy and radiation had robbed him of his strength, motivation and dignity. He'd suffered so much. It had almost been a blessing when he'd said his final "I love you" to her.

Almost. The loss of the man she had loved for decades would never leave her soul. Her heart would always bear that scar. Brian was no longer here. That was her new reality. And he would insist she did not wallow in grief and moved on. And she was. Viv was even ready to start dating. And had thought she'd snagged that first date earlier this morning.

Not really a date. More like another chance meeting. But planned. Less chance and more... Heck. She shook her head. That chance was obliterated now.

She wandered toward the greenhouse doors. Too bad he was a jerk. A handsome angry jerk. Who had also lost his partner.

Poor guy. She would cut him some slack. But this was not over. She had only just begun to manifest her dream job. Viv was not prepared to go down without a fight.

With a glance over her shoulder to the climbing monstera that had stretched its nearly two-foot-long yellow and white leaves to the glass ceiling in a quest to take over the room, she knew exactly which card she would play. Steeling her determination, she aimed toward the foyer.

Monsieur Ricard strode out from the kitchen as Viviane neared. He was taller than her by a head, and she stepped back from his overwhelming presence. He was no longer in a rage, but she could sense he was still off. She felt horrible for intruding on his—

No. Stick to the plan, Viv. You must keep this job.

"Coral is incommunicado," he offered with a splay of his hand. Then he jabbed it at his hip, which shoved back the suit coat. Businessman, for sure, Viv decided. And in need of relaxation. A quiet evening to shrug off the day's challenges. Not a battle with a stranger.

But…

"I can't abandon my work," Viv blurted out. "The plant that is climbing the south exterior wall needs to be removed immediately or it could cause structural damage. There's already a crack in one of the ceiling windowpanes."

After looking ready to protest, Rezin suddenly shifted from evident anger to genuine concern. "Really?"

Sensing him waver, Viv eased in further. "I called a rental place earlier. They will deliver a tall ladder tomorrow. I really shouldn't cancel. There's no telling how quickly that crack will spread and then you'll need to replace the entire glass pane. Who knows? The entire ceiling could come down."

A bit dramatic—the ceiling was well-supported with an iron framework—but it felt like a deal-closer.

Rezin rubbed his jaw, where the dark stubble was thicker this evening than it had been this morning. It gave the suited businessman a rebel look. Like he was all business during the day, but after he stepped out of the officc… Watch out! Viv had always been a sucker for rebels. Brian, who had grown up on a dairy farm, had been as straight and narrow as men were forged. *Marry for stability, save fantasies for just that.*

"Fine," he finally said. "Remove that one plant. And take photographs of the damage for me."

"I will do that. If you text me your details I'll send you photos as soon as I take them."

He gave her his number and she entered it in her contacts. Yes! She'd won that battle.

"You have until I can reach Coral," he said. "Where are you sleeping?"

Now he wanted to know her sleeping arrangements? How quickly the man's interests swerved. Rebel, indeed.

"Viviane?" he prompted.

Tugged from a delightful foray into imagining sleeping with a sexy Frenchman, Viv straightened. "Uh… Down the hall." She pointed over a shoulder. "Where Coral said I should stay."

"*Bien.* The servants' quarters."

"It is? Oh. It's such a beautiful room. With a large attached bathroom." Soaking in the bathtub with a goblet of wine in hand… She had already been working the Parisian lifestyle. "But if this is your home, I'd hate to impose. I suppose I could find a hotel room—" She didn't have the budget for a hotel room. *Pivot, Viv!* "But I promise I won't be in your way, Monsieur Ricard. Coral really didn't mention you living here."

"I don't live here. I need a place to crash while my penthouse is being renovated."

"Well, I'm sure you'll stay in one of the many bedrooms on the second or third floor. Not that I've been snooping, but I did look around when I first arrived. It's a beautiful mansion. Luxurious.

And the garden can be restored to its natural lush, yet tamed, state. It's actually in much better condition—"

Rez thrust up his palm. "Just remove the problem you mentioned, then cease all other work in the conservatory. I don't require such work. I'll get it straightened out with Coral. You will be properly compensated for the inconvenience. Understand?"

"I do." Darn! She was not prepared to walk away from this job. "But it might take a few days to carefully remove the monstera and clean up. I want to save as much of the plant as possible. It's remarkably hardy and can be propagated—" The man's growing sneer stifled her rambling. "But, like I said, I won't get in your way."

He huffed and checked his phone, perhaps scrolling to Coral's number and texting, because he'd started typing something in.

"I'll...uh..." Viv gestured toward the kitchen. "Grab something to eat and go to my room for the night. I head out in the mornings for a walk— Oh."

He tilted his head, giving her his complete attention. They were both thinking about their encounter. Or she hoped his memory had been jogged and he was feeling a modicum of guilt for being so hard-headed right now. On the other hand, she couldn't read his oh-so-blue eyes and suspected he was still seething but controlled it well. Yes, he seemed like a control freak to her.

"Guess the date is off, eh?" she tried. Her wince was quickly hidden with a bow of her head.

"The date?"

"Tomorrow morning at the *pâtisserie*? I mean, another chance meeting."

Oh, heck… When would she learn to keep her mouth shut?

"Ah. That."

Viv's heart raced as she waited for him to say *No worries…it was all a misunderstanding. Let's make up for it over Opera cakes and coffee.*

"Right. I have a lot of work in the morning," he said. *"Bonsoir, madame."*

He turned and headed toward the stairway.

Madame… Was that the French form of address for a widow? Or did she revert back to *mademoiselle* after losing her husband?

Viv hated being called a widow. The word was always delivered with a sad face. She was still young, alive, and had half her life ahead of her. She intended to live to one hundred. She was determined not to wither, play bingo on Tuesday nights, and grow a cat collection.

A new journey had begun in this Parisian mansion owned by this gruff yet handsome man. Viv was going to take that journey.

And be successful at it.

The next morning Rez leaned over his desk, fingers curling into fists. His son, Jean-Louis, whom he'd not expected to see in the office today, stood on the other side of the Louis XV desk that had been in the family since the inception of Le Beau.

Jean-Louis was going on about how he wanted Rez to go for a check-up with a doctor. What he wasn't saying, but had certainly implied, was that the doctor he wanted his dad to see was a psychiatrist.

His son had been suggesting he seek further medical help since the day Rez had left the hospital, but within the last few months his son's dedication to that concern had annoyingly veered toward Rez's mental health. Of course, he knew Jean-Louis had his best interests in mind, but he wasn't crazy!

"It's been a rough couple of years." Jean-Louis smoothed a palm down his lapel. He'd inherited his father's zeal for a fitted suit and diamonds at his cuffs. "You never take a break from work, Papa."

"I am perfectly capable. Especially here." Rez tapped his temple.

Why must they even have this absurd conversation? He was not mentally unsound. The memory loss episodes he experienced were few and far between.

"I have been CEO of Le Beau since I was twenty-eight. I know every aspect of the business from the acquisition of gemstones and fine metals to the design and marketing. I know each client by name and family. And I've been invited to more weddings than is believable. I *am* Le Beau. You will get your chance to sit in this chair in time, Jean-Louis. I promise you that."

Jean-Louis scoffed. "You think I want to steal the company out from under you? It's not like that. Papa, I am worried about your mental health. You forget things."

"You know that's a result of my brain injury."

"Yes—not your fault. But it must be watched. You require regular medical check-ups. And what about your dizzy spells? You collided with Penelope last week."

He'd not *collided* with Penelope, their receptionist/personal assistant. Caught by a sudden wave of dizziness, Rez had simply stepped wrong, and Penelope had been near him. He'd steadied himself by grasping her forearm. Not a big concern.

"Are you spying on me?" he asked.

"*Papa!* I'm in the office often. Penelope and I are great friends."

Jean-Louis was the principal buyer for Le Beau. Three-quarters of the year he traveled the world. The majority of his flights landed him in Amsterdam, the city of diamonds, and the key diamond center any successful jeweler must navigate like the back of his hand. When Rez had been hospitalized for two months following the accident that had taken his wife's life, it had been Jean-Louis who had overseen Le Beau.

His son had suggested Penelope for the assistant position, and Rez had been grateful to gain such a smart, efficient employee. She also brought in homemade croissants brushed with honey butter. Often.

"You don't know *me*," Rez said. He settled in the chair and shoved his hands over his hair. "I'm not ready to retire."

"Ready has nothing to do with this, Papa. *Uff!*" Jean-Louis checked his watch. "The client is due in moments."

"Yes, I do know that," Rez said defensively. "I've had the meeting scheduled for weeks." His watch sent him a reminder an hour before all important meetings. Without that crutch, he might not remember. "If you will leave us to discuss the design they want for their wedding set…?"

"I'm going to sit in on this consultation." Jean-Louis leaned against the brick wall, arms crossed over his chest. The Picasso painting hung on the wall next to him had been purchased by Rez's father in the sixties. "The client has requested I do so."

Rez's jaw dropped open. Had the client requested his son's presence out of the blue? Or had Jean-Louis encouraged the client to include him? At the very least, Penelope should have alerted him to his addition to the meeting.

"I am perfectly capable—" Rez started.

"Today's meeting has nothing to do with your

mental capacity," Jean-Louis said. "And I would never say as much to any of the clientele. You can trust that our family secrets are safe, Papa."

Family secrets? They had no secrets. They were a family of father and son, grieving over a lost mother and wife. Very well, Rez did not want his condition to be known. He'd not told Penelope about his memory loss or dizzy spells, but he suspected Jean-Louis might have done so. His limp was an obvious fact; he couldn't hide that.

"This client wants innovative ideas," Jean-Louis added. "The Prince is marrying an American hip-hop singer. So…"

Inwardly, Rez rolled his eyes. Why had they come to Le Beau if they wanted bling? *Ugh.* He hated that word. He despised the hideous creations that hung around necks on red carpets and in music videos. Thick, gold, and massive amounts of diamonds.

Rationally, he knew it would be a relevant step for Le Beau to make. To add celebrity endorsements. To offer "bling." To appeal to the younger generation. But, as well, Rez felt sure his great-grandfather would turn over in his grave should such a travesty manifest itself.

The intercom buzzed, and Penelope announced she would show in the clients.

Rez stood abruptly and winced, catching his palm on the desk to maintain balance. He'd had pins in his thigh to hold the bones together while they mended for six months. Now what remained was a thick scar from hip to knee. Never knowing if his leg would support him made him feel incapable. But he was not. A man did not need two good legs to run a billion-dollar jewelry empire. And he still wielded the mental capacity to control and run the business that meant everything to him.

Most days he did, anyway.

Rez tightened his jaw. The thought of losing control of the company was terrifying. It was all he had left.

"Papa?" His son had seen his reaction to the pain.

"I'm fine. Let's do this, then."

Viv dumped the can of whole yellow tomatoes into a bowl. Sliding her hands into the cool goo, she broke up the tomatoes with her fingers. She had forgotten how the sensual art of cooking made her feel. Connected to something that she could create. Reawakened by scents, textures, and flavors. Almost like her gardening, but creating sustenance. And love. Food, she'd realized early in her marriage, was her love language.

Since Brian's death she rarely cooked for herself. Yes, she'd not shown herself proper love. Food came from a box, frozen, or was picked up in the drive-through. Not the healthiest way to eat, but she'd let nutrition slip from her self-care ritual. Along with many things, such as dressing up and wearing make-up, reading a thick historical novel, going for walks, even the occasional weekend of binge-watching a TV series.

That she was cooking for the handsome, yet prickly owner of this fabulous mansion brightened her smile. Was she plying her seductive culinary skills on him? Hardly. This was a simple lasagna.

With the tomatoes sufficiently crushed, she rinsed her hands, then seasoned the sauce and mixed in the sautéed onions, along with finely diced zucchini and mushrooms. No meat. She wasn't a vegetarian, but she didn't know if Rezin was a meat-eater. Now to layer it with the cooked noodles, along with lots of fresh mozzarella and ricotta. The cheese shop down the street was remarkable. She would never buy pre-packaged cheese again.

Admiring the assembled dish, she tried to remember when she'd last made lasagna for Brian. He had eaten anything and everything she'd made. Always complimented her on it. Most hardworking men were thankful for a home-cooked meal after a long day.

A wistful heaviness landed in her heart. The feeling was strange. Almost as if she were cheating on the ghost of her marriage with tomato sauce and hand-torn cheese.

"Oh, don't be silly," she quietly admonished herself out loud.

And yet a tear blossomed. Sniffling, she closed her eyes. How odd...the things that tugged at her grief. Lasagna, of all things. She certainly hoped she'd be able to sit across the table from Rezin and eat it without shedding a tear.

That was *if* he accepted her meal as a peace offering. She had no idea when he would return to the mansion this evening. And likely he preferred fancy French cuisine.

Placing the pan in the oven, she set a timer on her phone.

Now to do some sweeping.

Viv was determined to make the conservatory ready for when she won the approval to work on its entirety. Because no matter what, she must win it.

Rez stormed over the mansion's threshold and slammed the door behind him. He had been muttering to himself during the entire ride from work to home. Now, away from the office, he was free to let loose.

He swore. Punched the air. "Jean-Louis had no right! Trying to make me seem feeble... And that ridiculous design!"

The Scandinavian Prince had settled on a rose gold setting with extremely large diamonds. Too many of them for taste and elegance. And the fussy Asscher cut he'd requested—reminiscent of the Art Deco style—did not properly suit the contemporary setting.

When had he lost connection with his son so that—? *Hell.*

Rez blew out his breath.

He and Jean-Louis had never been close. Colette had been his son's best friend. Rez was his father—a kind one, but also an exacting teacher who had always demanded the best as Jean-Louis navigated his way into the company. Emotionally, he might never embrace his son, or even think to pat him on the back. It wasn't what the Ricard men did. They provided for their families. They were respected community members. They showed their love with action, not emotion.

And they never disrespected their fathers by trying to shove them out of the company.

Swearing again, Rez limped toward the kitchen, but his anger got the better of him again as he recalled his living situation.

"Can't even get comfortable in my own home. Have to stay in this…memory trap. Of all places! And with that strange woman in the garden."

"I am not strange."

The words came out defensively from behind him.

CHAPTER THREE

REZ SPUN TOWARD THE VOICE. A spritely face peered between a broom handle and a bundle of long bamboo spikes. Emerald eyes beamed from between lush lashes. A perfectly kissable mouth, held in tight concern, teased at his need to soften it. Yet capping the sweet face was a mess of tangled hair, struck through with a few of the spikes. And the dirt smeared on her cheeks further added to her strangeness quotient.

"Strange is…debatable." Rez gestured to her face.

That moment of taking her in had swept him down from his tirade. Since the accident, anger tended to strike without warning.

He breathed out.

Calm, Rez. You're not angry at her. You're angry at Coral for not telling you she would be here. Touching Colette's plants. Treading on your memories.

With his next deep, surrendering inhalation Rez caught a whiff of something delicious. "What is that?"

"Lasagna," she replied. "I thought the least I

could do was to feed you, since you're putting up with me staying here when you hadn't expected a guest."

It did smell delicious after a long day at work. During which he'd only bothered to drink coffee and down a *pain au chocolat* for lunch.

And yet... He would not be so easily distracted. "Was the ladder delivered? Did you complete the one task I allowed you?"

"The ladder was not delivered, so I wasn't able to attack the climbing menace. Tomorrow for sure. They promised. Maybe. That's what I understood from their blend of French and English."

"I doubt talking to them is how the dirt got on your face. I meant it when I forbade you from working in the garden."

"My work does involve dirt, *monsieur*. Sorry. No way around that one. I had to clear an area for the ladder."

He cleared his throat. Made a huffing dissatisfied noise. Again, Rez reminded himself not to take out his anger on this innocent American woman. That messy hair was appealing, in an odd, can-I-tidy-you-a-bit? way. The urge to reach over and brush the hair from her lashes twitched his fingers. And what was that about? Was he attracted to her? Could he be angry with her and want her at the same time?

Want her? Now he was thinking foolish thoughts.

No, he was a man! She was an attractive woman. Of course he entertained *ideas* about her.

"We'll discuss any concerns you may still have over dinner," she said, and walked away, swinging the broom at her side.

A bit too confident for a guest in his home. However, Rez rather liked it that she had not balked at his tirade. Yet he would not soften simply because he could imagine kissing her soft rose lips and raking his fingers through her messy hair.

Certainly not.

Very well. A discussion they would have. Over lasagna. He did enjoy Italian cuisine.

"Très bien," Rez said as he dished a second helping of lasagna onto his plate.

Viv beamed. She was pretty sure that meant very good. The compliment felt like a much-needed hug. Perhaps he understood her love language?

She did long for physical connection. With a man. But she should not fall into the fantasy of Rezin's sexiness again. Was it possible her menopausal hormones had somehow reverted to teenager level? It certainly felt like it. She almost sighed when she was gazing into his bluer-than-blue eyes.

"It is tasty, isn't it?" She made the save before embarrassing herself with the kind of lovey-dovey sigh that should only come out of the mouth of a schoolgirl. "I looked up the recipe on Pinterest."

Rez flashed her a look over his fork.

She shrugged. "My recipe book is at home in Minnesota. Lasagna is my go-to dish. I gathered the ingredients this morning on my walk. That little market a couple blocks away is awesome. I got fresh blueberries as well. Organic, even! I'm thinking about making syrup for pancakes in the morning."

"Crêpes?" Rez offered.

"Yes, of course. When in France, eh?"

She winked at him. Actually winked!

Viv quickly looked at her plate, forking up the noodles and tomato sauce. Had she really done such a thing? This flirting stuff was nerve-racking.

Was that what this was? Flirting? Oh, mercy. She was not ready for this.

But, yes—yes, she was. Maybe? Could she channel a teenager long enough to figure out how this stuff worked nowadays? It had been nearly thirty years since she'd flirted with a stranger. That made her feel ancient. But she was not!

"The dinner is lovely," Rez said.

Whew! Saved from her mental dive into decrepitude by a smoldering French baritone.

"The fact you're still working in my garden is not."

Viv set down her fork. She'd prepared for this argument while weeding through the desiccated undergrowth that edged the conservatory walls.

"You said you were going to talk to Coral about it?" she asked.

"She's still incommunicado. Coral does that. Goes off on soul-searching adventures for days, sometimes weeks."

"That sounds wonderful. This trip for me is a bit of a soul-searching mission."

She noticed his wince even though he tried to hide it behind a bite of food. They were not any sort of confidantes, and he could probably care little what her soul desired. Right. *Stay on task, Viv.*

"You should know that I've inspected the greenhouse and all the foliage over the past few days. Assessed what needs to get cleared out, what can be salvaged—"

"It will all remain untouched," he interrupted firmly. "You Americans have difficulty with the word *no.*"

"I take offense on behalf of all Americans," Viv said, but added a light tone. "Still, that plant must come down."

Rez leaned his elbows on the table. The man must be some kind of corporate raider, because he wielded the solemn stare and conviction that Viv imagined such a job required.

"The monstera," he said. "Is that what you called it?"

"Yes." It was a common plant, but it impressed her that he'd remembered.

"I had no idea plants could be so destructive."

"Well, they don't do it on purpose," she defended. "That particular plant can become a bit of a weed if it isn't tended often. And it's a weighty thing."

"As I've said, when that job is complete, so is your gardening refurbishment."

"If you say so."

But if—when—she got her way, things would go much differently.

Slow and easy, Viv. Don't spook the man.

She propped an elbow on the table and caught her cheek against her palm. "Are you okay?"

Setting down the wine goblet, he tilted his head. "Why would you ask such a thing?"

"You seemed upset when you arrived earlier. I know I can be a little strange. I have an affinity for tucking crystals in my bra, I'm distracted by cats and will hold complete conversations with them, and I also cry easily— Oh. Sorry. I also tend to ramble about odd things no one ever wants to hear. Anyway…." She tried a smile and got the tiniest curve of his mouth in return. "If it's me staying here that's upsetting you…"

"You have nothing to do with my earlier outburst. I do apologize for that. Sometimes I have to hold things in until I get home. I don't like to rage at the office. It's not that I rage. It's just…"

She could sense his need to change the subject. Who would want to talk about something like their anger?

"What *is* the office, actually?" She knew he was a jeweler; the pastry shop clerk had told her as much.

"I own Le Beau. The jewelers. We've been in business for a century."

"That's impressive. Is that the company I've heard about that caters to the rich and famous?"

"We cater to a certain elite clientele, *oui*. I am the CEO. I spend a lot of time on video chat with various vendors, and approving paperwork and contracts, but my favorite part of the job is designing."

"Really? You make fabulous necklaces and bracelets?"

"And rings and earrings and brooches. From the sketch on the page, to obtaining the fine gemstones and metals, to putting it all together. I am unique in this business, in that I like to immerse myself in the entire process. Unlike the CEOs of most jewelry companies, who send out all the work beyond the design, I don't hand off my creations to the cutters and setters. My reward is seeing my work adorn a woman's graceful neck or fingers."

"You must have designed for celebrities?"

"Many."

"Like who?"

"Some princes, an opera singer, royalty..." he casually offered.

"How is it that jewelry can make a man so furious? I mean, when you came in earlier..."

He clasped his hands before his chin and eyed her carefully. Blue eyes and daydreams teased Viv to lean forward, resting her chin on the back of her hand.

"My son arouses the fury in me," Rez said. "He has...certain ideas about the direction Le Beau should move in to stay relevant."

"You don't want to stay relevant?"

"We already are. That's all I'll say about that."

"Fair enough." Interfering in a family matter was not something she cared to do. And she cared little about celebrities and their quest for sparkly things. "More wine?"

"I'm good. But I'm also curious."

Something lightened in his expression; it changed his entire face. So much so, Viv felt herself lighten.

"Crystals in your bra?"

She'd *said* that? *Oh, Viv!*

"It's a thing. I love crystals. Minerals. Pretty stones. And a garnet worn against your heart invites warmth and love."

"I...don't know what to say to that."

"Well, you believe much the same, without even knowing it."

His eyebrow quirked. The man was too delicious. She could stare at him all evening.

"You design jewelry with precious stones. You

may not be aware of the qualities each stone attracts, but they do."

"So, garnets for love? I'll remember that," Rez said. "Thank you for the meal. Now I should retire. I've some notes to make for work tomorrow." He rose and smoothed a hand down his tie. *"Bonsoir, madame."*

Rez left the room, his hand gliding along the wall as he did so. As if for balance?

"Goodnight!" she called. "I promise to only touch the monstera tomorrow."

Her line of vision followed him to the stairwell, where he slapped a palm on the newel post and paused. Was that a wince? The man really did allow his anger to get to him. That was not good for anyone's health. Poor guy. He needed a hug.

But she couldn't simply walk up and hug him. That was intrusive. And, as a certified introvert with only brief moments of regretful extroversion, not her thing. Rez was still a stranger. And, apparently, she was strange.

I'll take that. She smiled. Better to be strange and still have a job than be kicked out on her keister.

From the pocket of her chinos she dug out the small crystal she'd purchased while on her morning walk. Moonstone. The creamy white stone blinked bright blue when she tilted it. Flashy, yet hiding so many more secrets. It reminded her of Paris.

And, yes, the garnet in her bra was for love. But

also it was a very sexy stone. She *did* want to get her sexy on. And boy, oh, boy, she knew of an eligible bachelor who would help her.

Leaning back on the chair and crossing her legs, she eyed the lasagna. When Rez had disappeared from her sight, she dished up another helping.

In his room, Rez slipped off his coat, shoes, loosened his tie, and sat on the end of the king-sized bed.

Relevant. Had he actually used that word? Of course Le Beau was relevant. And Jean-Louis would never convince him otherwise.

He tossed his dark tie onto the light counterpane. Everything in this room, from walls to furnishings and fabrics, was a soft cream color. Plain. He liked color when he could control the combinations, the moods. Setting colored gemstones was one of his favorite things to do. It was a fine art.

He was aware that gemstones had been assigned certain qualities, attributes, and even emotional resonance. Bunch of nonsense, that stuff. But garnet for warmth and love?

"More than warmth and love," he muttered. "It's sexy and passionate."

Stretching his arms over his head, he tilted his head from side to side. That had been a delicious meal. Certainly beat frozen dinners from the supermarket.

And Viviane was not so difficult to converse

with. Even if she did seem snoopy. He would not normally reveal anything about his family troubles to a stranger.

If structural damage could be caused by that overgrown plant then he certainly wanted that taken care of—and quickly. So she'd be around another day or two.

He'd survive the intrusion. After all, she was a beautiful woman. She'd cleaned up nicely for dinner. Not a dirt smudge to be seen. Her hair was a certain shade he couldn't decide on. Rose-blonde? Pale copper? It was bright…gleaming. It framed her heart-shaped face. And her curiosity didn't offend him so much as intrigue him. She was simple, down-to-earth—quite literally—and…

And the complete opposite to Colette. Not at all fussy or self-aware to a fault, as his wife had been. He'd loved Colette, even when she'd selfishly demanded his constant reassurance of her beauty, her agelessness, her appeal.

Rez glanced at his reflection in the mirror across the room. He'd learned to make those assurances by rote. They had grown to mean little to him. A woman needn't cater to anyone to gain acceptance. All women were beautiful in their own way. And now, with a splash of fresh air in the form of a strange gardener, his interest had been piqued.

"I could get to know her," he said aloud, his mood daring to lighten.

He was a single man. And a man had needs. Like touch, conversation, and sex. And Viviane was staying in his home. So close. Sexy and passionate…just like the gemstone.

Was he ready to have another go at dating? Simply get closer to a woman? And, if so, might he have a fling with the gardener?

The fact he was considering it proved his broken heart wasn't completely shattered. He was a living, breathing, wanting man. And it was about time he started acting like one.

CHAPTER FOUR

THE LADDER WAS to be delivered before noon. Viv decided to take a quick walk around the neighborhood, starting with her favorite *pâtisserie*. She'd stepped outside the mansion and turned to pull the door shut when Rez appeared and walked out.

A nice surprise to see him. But she crushed a few proverbial eggshells while they strolled to the main sidewalk. What sort of mood was he in? They'd come to terms over her working on the one plant, but he was still adamant that was all she'd touch. And he'd dismissed her when she'd sort of suggested they do the bakery date.

"Are you off to work?" she asked gaily. "Designing jewelry?"

"Yes. I've a long day ahead of me."

He opened the wrought-iron gate and she walked through. The sunlight glowed like fire. It caught in Rez's eyes and glinted. Like some kind of fairytale prince.

Silly, Viv.

And yet they were both here. And her destination was close.

"Want to change your mind about walking to the *pâtisserie* with me?" she asked. "My treat. I'm sure they've a good supply of Opera cakes this early in the morning."

Rez winced and glanced to the street. Only then did Viv notice the black limousine parked there. Oh. His driver?

"While I'd love to walk with you," he said, and his tone sounded genuine, "as I've said...work."

"Oh, of course."

What did she know about the rich and obviously entitled? He probably took a chauffeur everywhere. And his stylish leather dress shoes certainly were not walk-wear.

Suddenly Rez leaned in and bussed one of her cheeks. A kiss? So soon? Should she turn her head into it or—? Oh. Viv realized the man was doing the French thing. When he moved to her opposite cheek she fought the urge to tilt her head and bring their mouths closer and let the common French means of saying farewell happen.

The brisk contact thrilled her. Perhaps he didn't completely hate her?

"I woke up wondering something," he said with a touch of lightness.

"Good dreams, eh? What were you wondering?"

He chuckled. "What sort of crystal you might have tucked in your bra today."

When she tried to meet his gaze he looked to the side. Embarrassed? He'd woken up with *that* on his mind? Viviane tugged in the corner of her lower lip.

"Sorry, that was forward…" he said.

"Moonstone," she rushed out. "It's a piece I picked up from a shop in the Louvre the second day I was here. It reminds me of Paris."

"Is that so? Moonstone…" He considered it, then nodded. "Appropriate. *Au revoir, madame,*" he said. "The ladder arrives today?"

"Yes—er…*oui.* Don't worry, I promise only to do the necessary work. You have a good day."

Viv watched the limo pull away from the curb. She smoothed her cheek where the heat of his touch lingered. Burnished to a rosy warmth by the brush of his stubble.

"Nice…" she whispered.

Ten minutes later she had selected the Opera cake, and also a half-dozen *macarons.* When she dug out cash to pay, the clerk—the same one who had served her yesterday morning—waved her hand.

"*Non, madame.* Monsieur Ricard has covered it."

"What?"

The clerk nodded enthusiastically. "All your purchases are paid for. Always."

Tapping the ten-euro note against her lower lip, Viv took that in. What a nice gesture. Rezin Ricard was a gentleman. Who had almost…sort of…kissed her out front of the mansion.

She knew it hadn't been a kiss in the romantic aspect, but she was going with it for as long as his heat remained on her skin. And, yes, she could still feel him there...so close.

"Madame?"

Right. No place to daydream.

Viv took the bag of pastries and walked outside. Could an American woman, out of place in her life, and precariously balancing a line to a new path, dare to dream about getting closer to a handsome Frenchman who might also be walking the emotion-laden line that grief and loss tended to draw?

"Why not?" she muttered aloud, and then walked toward the Tuileries Garden, her steps much bouncier than usual.

Sitting in the back of his limo, Rez massaged his leg. Today the pain in his leg pierced him as if with a steel poker. He'd had to grit his teeth while talking to Viviane.

When he'd bussed her cheeks it had been a means to hide his wince. But in those seconds he'd drawn in her scent. Sweet, with a hint of green. Like foliage and candy. Subtle, yet delicious. Naturally erotic.

Thinking about the luscious aroma rising from her skin averted the pain. The utter freshness of Viviane was a unique and refreshing swerve from Colette's uptight perfectionism.

More than anything, he would have loved to stroll alongside Viv. Chat. Get to know her better. Thank her again for the delicious supper.

But although little things slipped his mind, he never forgot to check his calendar. And this morning it had reminded him of a video call with Sven Stellian, to go over the next few months of mining projects. Sven was the mastermind behind Le Beau's precious metals. He appreciated decades-old whiskey from Scotland. Rez made sure the man received a good supply every Christmas.

Hours later, Rez signed off with Sven. He closed the mining file on his computer and—the entire screen went blank. What the hell…? With a flutter, the screen blinked back to life and showed the open page where the mining file had been but was not anymore.

Gritting his jaw, Rez tapped a few keys. The file had been there. He wasn't computer illiterate. He knew how to find and open files and save backups and…

He swore. He must have hit delete. It was the only explanation for the missing file. With a sigh, he slouched into his chair. Were Jean-Louis's concerns true? *Was* he losing it mentally? Even to consider it made Rez's stomach lurch. His brain had been damaged in the accident. The doctors had said he'd have to live with this new normal. But they'd not said he'd get worse.

"Monsieur Ricard?" Penelope peeked in the

open doorway of his office. Her bright red hair was coiled into a forties-style updo. "How did the meeting go?"

Rez exhaled. "Penelope, I need your help."

Fifteen minutes later the file was restored, and the changes Rez had made during his conversation with Sven remained.

"*Merci*, Penelope. You just…" *Saved my ass.* "Made my day."

"Not a problem. Thanks to the linked computer system, I do backups of all your files. Please don't think I'm overstepping."

"Absolutely not. You are a valuable employee. Some days I would be lost without you."

She shrugged, and then paused on her way out from his office. "If you don't mind my saying… I care for you like a father, Monsieur Ricard. You mustn't think Jean-Louis is out to get you."

He'd not realized that Jean-Louis and Penelope shared such intimate details. But perhaps she was just perceptive. The woman did have a way of always knowing when he'd need coffee, or arriving with files for a project minutes before he thought to ask for them.

He knew Jean-Louis was not out to get him. Rez just liked to maintain control. And control over Le Beau was one of very few things he actually could still manage.

"Your perspective is different than mine, Penelope. But I do thank you for your concern."

She should not concern herself with his personal life. But he wouldn't say that. She meant well.

"Shall I bring you some croissants for lunch?" she asked. "I made them this morning."

"With honey butter?"

She nodded enthusiastically. "I'll be right back."

Croissants would see him through an afternoon of paperwork. Yet the idea of returning to the mansion prodded at him. An intriguing woman occupied his home. Her scent still teased at him with the crook of a finger and a quirky smile.

She'd be gone soon enough. And then he would be alone.

And, since Viviane had crashed into his life, being alone no longer appealed to Rez.

CHAPTER FIVE

ANOTHER FAVORITE DISH of Viviane's was quiche. Baked until the crispy pale brown crust ruffled at the edges. Bits of ham and Emmental cheese added a savory touch. Her mother had passed along the recipe to her.

Raised by a single mom who'd never had a desire to marry, Viviane had garnered independence and necessary life skills by observing and following her mother's actions. When she'd passed away eight years ago from old age—her mother hadn't had Viv until she was forty—it had felt natural, blessed, and like she was moving on to something bigger and better.

Violet Westberg had lived her life exactly as she'd desired and had regretted nothing. Viv believed her mom would be proud of her setting off on this new life adventure.

"You don't have to cook for me every night." Rez sat down before the table. "Although…"

Viv sat across from him. "Although?"

"My next thought was that I hope you don't take that statement seriously. This smells *incroyable*."

The look on his face told her she'd scored another win. While cooking to seduce wasn't part of her master plan to keep her job here, it wasn't a terrible side hustle in winning the man's trust.

"I don't mind cooking for two," she said. "I have to make something for myself. I might as well double it for you. As long as you don't mind me tooling around in your kitchen? I know you'd rather not have me in your home at all."

"On the contrary. It's the garden."

"So, you don't mind me traipsing about the rest of the place?"

"Traipsing?"

"You know… Floundering. Meandering. Generally wandering."

He chuckled. "Until I can reach Coral you are welcome here."

"And when you do reach her? Then I'm out on my behind?"

He didn't answer, instead sipped his wine.

"I'm voting for Coral to win the struggle," Viv said. "I've already lost my heart to the garden. There are half a dozen varieties of fern, most still very salvageable. And the hostas! Anyway, I want to start at the top and work on the monstera and take propagatable shoots when I can. I climbed to the top of the ladder before you arrived, while the delivery man was still here. I was able to get some good shots of the cracked glass pane while I was up there."

"Can you send them to me?"

"I already did. Check your texts after we eat."

He patted his jacket pocket but didn't take out his cell phone. Good call.

"Do you feel safe climbing the ladder with no one around?" he asked.

His genuine concern buoyed her. "Yes, it's very sturdy. And the delivery man did me a favor by anchoring it mid-climb to a supporting beam on the outer conservatory wall. As well, he included a safety harness."

"Your profession seems quite specific. Refurbishing indoor gardens? Do you get a lot of work?"

"As I've explained, it's a new business model I'm creating. I'm an award-winning horticulturist, so I've got the skills. I also worked in landscaping for the last two decades, so I do know the lay of the land, so to speak. I published a book ten years ago, titled *The Plant Whisperer*."

He wrinkled a brow. "You…whisper to plants?"

She chuckled. "Sometimes. Talking to plants releases humidity into the air and they thrive on that. Anyway, I was even on *Good Morning America* to promote the book. It was fun. But I suspect my fifteen minutes of fame never made it across the ocean to France."

"Why is it that you are here in France and not America?"

"That's all part of the plan. I want to work in Europe. Travel. Experience the world while making a living. I can create an entire garden from scratch in a pre-existing space, or revive an ill-cared-for garden. I think I mentioned I want to call it either Glass Houses or The Plant Whisperer? What do you think when you hear those titles?"

"'Glass Houses' sounds too narrow. You want to be able to work with clients who may not have their garden under glass. There are a lot of terrace gardens in Paris and other European cities."

"You're right. I'll let Harley know. The Plant Whisperer it is. Harley is my marketing pro, who works with me remotely. She's currently reviving my social media and I send her photos daily. She's very good at what she does. I plan to employ only women. We *are* the nurturers, growers and keepers, after all."

"Bold…"

Viv eyed the man over her wine goblet. He met her gaze with those gorgeous blues. The connection felt electric. Longer than a glance, for sure. Was she interpreting it correctly—that he was interested in her—or had it simply been too long since she'd made simple eye contact with a man?

Reading a man's thoughts had never been her forte, even while she was married.

"I like a woman who goes for what she wants," Rez said. "Strength is attractive."

Now she blushed.

Oh, Viv, there's no sign of strength in flushed cheeks.

She glanced aside. Why was it so difficult to

accept a compliment from this man without reading more into it? Did he find her attractive? Like, enough for dating? A real kiss? Romance?

No, it was a figure of speech, obviously. Maybe… Oh, God, *could* he be attracted to her?

"Thank you," she finally said. "Are you finished? I'll wash up the dishes."

"I'll help. I like talking to you," Rez said. "And this will extend the conversation."

"I like talking to you, too. You're my first Frenchman."

"Is that so? First in what way?"

She caught his husky intonation. Mercy, if the man knew that the mere sound of a French accent made her melt.

"In every way. Talking to. Cooking for. Living with. We are, in a manner, living together."

"So we are. You…have a thing for Frenchmen?"

"Honestly?"

Did she dare? Why not? She was a grown woman. The time to couch her sentiments with care and be wary of putting her truth out there was in the past. This was her new life. Viviane Westberg would not shrink from adventure.

"How could any woman not? The French language is melodious, and so sexy. And you've got this voice…" She handed him a plate and, with no more dishes to wash, turned her hip against the sink to watch him.

"This voice?" He set the plate on the counter.

"It touches me. My skin," she added. Since it didn't seem to be freaking her out, she settled into the flirtation. "But I bet you get that all the time. When you walk down the street all the women swoon, right?"

Rez chuckled deeply—and there was that resonant tone that glided across her skin like a lover's touch.

He suddenly paused and gave her a look. "Seriously?" he asked.

Caught! She shrugged. "It's the truth."

"I don't walk down the street very often. Not lately, with my leg acting up."

"I noticed you favor it. Have you been in an accident?"

Rez turned his hip toward the sink to face her. "Yes. The injury is a couple of years old." He eased a hand down his thigh.

"Does it hurt all the time?" she asked.

"Some days I don't even notice it. Other days it's always there. Not excruciating, but enough to distract me."

"Do you take medication for it?"

"Painkillers?" He shook his head. "Not into drugs. The neighbor who lives on the ground floor of my building in the Sixth brings me teas that she's concocted from her garden. I have no idea what herbs are in them. Some of them taste awful. But they do alleviate the pain."

He sat on the chair before the table and stretched

out his leg. He probably didn't want her to see his wince, but she did.

Viv walked over and touched his hair, then bowed to kiss his forehead. A real kiss. Not a genial bussing of the cheeks in a farewell kiss.

"I know that won't make it better, but it's something my mother always did for me. I was thinking about her as I was cooking. She was so nurturing." Viv pulled her fingers from his oh-so-soft hair. "Sorry. That was— I shouldn't have... I sort of just reacted with that kiss." It had been something she'd always done for her husband, too.

Rez closed his eyes. "React all you like. I think that kiss may have been as restorative as herbal tea. Why don't you try another here?" He tapped his cheek.

Really? Their light flirtation had taken on a suggestive tone. Her muscles loosened and her jaw softened. Butterflies invaded her heart. Nerves? When was the last time she'd stood so close to a man who was not her husband? And had him suggest she kiss him?

Too long. Pre-marriage long. It would only hurt to start counting by decades.

But she wanted this. Felt sure she was ready to take this step. Diving back into the dating pool was on her shortlist. It was now or never.

She bent to kiss Rez's cheek. Leather and wine scented his aura. Solid and sure. His presence silently reassured while also teasing her closer. The brush of her lips against his stubble startled her.

In the next moment she kissed his cheek quickly, then pulled back and met his gaze. A kiss to take away the pain? Or something so much more? "Better?"

"I think so. I... Uh..."

Viv swallowed. Something in his gaze grasped her, held her, but gently, and with a seeking innocence.

"Do you want to give me another?" He tapped his lips. "Here?"

Oh, did she! And yet....

Tilting her head, Viv did not move away from him, but she did not kiss him. Because her heartbeats thundered. Because his gaze still challenged her to make the next move. Because...

"I'm not sure I remember *how* to kiss a man." The words spilled off her tongue. The truth. A silly confession. "It's been so long."

"A person doesn't forget how to kiss."

"I think I may have."

"The one to my forehead and cheek felt right."

Yes, and logically if she kissed his mouth it would require the same movement and bravery. Truthfully, she'd not forgotten the mechanics of such an intimate act. But she couldn't tell him that. And she really did want to feel his mouth...

Closing her eyes, Viv leaned in, taking her time.

Nervous anticipation made her fingers shake and her breaths shallow.

Yes, you remember. You can do this.

Rez's scent subtly spiced the air. His soft breaths lured her. Should she tilt her head? Definitely keep her eyes closed. But part her lips slightly? Or keep a closed mouth? She couldn't remember the rules of a first kiss!

Viv, just…react.

Heartbeats pounding a path toward a cliff, she made contact. Soft, warm mouths. Breaths entwining. A gentle connection. She hadn't missed the target.

Stop thinking about what can go wrong.

Pressing more firmly, Viv moved into the kiss. Rez's hand slid up her back, reassuring, holding her there. His heat surprised her, while also melting her inhibitions.

Yes, this was okay.

It was more than okay. It felt different. New. Yet not so new. She'd done this a thousand times before. Muscle memory took over. Actually, it felt right. Nothing wrong with this. She was a woman kissing a man. A man who had asked her to kiss him.

Take some more if you dare.

So she did dare.

Stubble tickled her chin. A brisk brush of masculinity. Viv deepened the kiss, taking what she had craved for so long, but hadn't been aware she was missing. This, she needed. This abandon. This sharing of desire. This feeling of being wanted. Tasted. Touched.

He kissed her in return. No signs of pulling away. He wanted it as much as she did. Both his hands held her—one at her back, the other clutching her hip. He did not demand. He accepted. And gave back.

The soft wet heat of their mingling tongues sent shivers down her spine and tingled across her skin. Butterflies swirled in her core. She slid a hand along his stubble-roughened jaw and threaded her fingers into his soft, dark hair. Holding him. Telling him what she wanted with her mouth. Taking whatever he would give her.

And when she felt him pull away, his gemstone blue eyes searched hers. A smile quirked his mouth. And this time he kissed her. She slid a leg along his hip and sat on his lap. He bracketed her head with his strong, powerful hands. Kissing her deeply, lingering, tasting her. Finding her.

He moaned. A deep, throaty resonance that vibrated in her core.

And then something changed.

Viv sat back, tugging in her lip with a tooth. The sound of his pleasure had inexplicably slammed on the brake. She touched her mouth. A tiny "Oh!" escaped. And then…"I…uh…"

She stood and pressed her hands over her pounding heart. The hard outline of the moonstone and her nipple rubbed her palm. The kiss had been okay. It had to be. Right?

And yet… Guilt rose. What had she just done? She had sat on the man's lap! And he wasn't even her husband!

"I need to be away… Right now. Because… uh…" She fumbled to explain her conflicting thoughts. And then gave up.

Viv rushed out of the kitchen, aiming for the quiet room in which she was being allowed to stay. Closing the door behind her, she ran to the bed and slumped down on the floor before it, her back hitting the mattress and wood frame. Catching her head in her hands, she tried to fend off tears, but it was too late.

She swore softly. Closed her eyes and shook her head.

What are you doing, Viv?

Maybe she wasn't as ready to dive in as she'd thought.

Rez tilted back his head and closed his eyes. The taste of Viviane lingered in his mouth. Wine and quiche. And the sexy surprise of her settling onto his lap and forgetting herself in that incredible kiss. She had not forgotten how to do it, that was for sure. And, holding her in his arms, he had felt the pain slip away. So had the grief.

In that moment he'd shared intimacy with Viv, he'd not thought about Colette. And he hadn't been struck by lightning or been wailed at by a disgruntled spirit.

It was all right to move onward, to invite a new woman into his life. It would never be easy. He would always bear the guilt. And he could relate to that look Viv had given him when she'd pulled away. That moment of uncertainty. Of wondering if it was truly right to move forward. Begin again.

He didn't fault her for running away. And he wouldn't chase after her. He couldn't.

When would it get easier? He wanted to be comfortable kissing a woman again, touching her body, having sex. He needed that contact. Craved it. And he desired Viv. But he didn't want to scare her away or tread on any tender threads that still tethered her to her husband. Because he could relate to that emotional bondage.

The only way this could work— Well, he hadn't a clue. But he didn't want to give up. Not this time. Something about Viv made him want to try.

But was it possible right now, with his life the way it was? He had enough to contend with, dodging Jean-Louis's demands he see a psychiatrist.

Viv was a life buoy that he wanted to grasp, but it felt as if the tides were pushing him further away from safety.

CHAPTER SIX

THE NEXT MORNING Viv did not head for the kitchen, where she heard Rez brewing coffee. After last night's kiss, she wasn't sure where she stood with him. And first thing in the morning was not her best time for confrontations.

So she veered toward the conservatory and took a few more photos. She forwarded those to Harley, her "Mistress of Marketing."

Harley had given herself that title. They'd been friends for a decade, and she was a master of social media, creating and maintaining websites, and pinpointing marketing angles. Viv was only one of her many clients. At the moment she lived in Viv's apartment. After breaking up with a boyfriend, Harley had had to move fast, and the timing had worked perfectly for her to take up the rent on Viv's place.

After a sign-off to Harley, Viv then climbed up the ladder, garden clippers hooked at her utility belt, to begin the heavy pruning. It was all she could do with the short rein Rez had given her regarding work. It would take a few days if she took her time and was careful.

She'd fallen asleep last night after a long shower. Her dramatic escape following The Kiss had been just that. Drama. She was over it now. Mostly. Pulled in two directions, her heart was not so much having a difficult time with the introduction of a love interest, but rather taking its time adjusting. *Was* Rez a love interest? Or had it merely been flirtation? A moment when they'd both dropped their guard?

She didn't know how to label it. Nor how to label that moment of panic when she'd realized she was sitting on a man's lap.

It had been nearly thirty years since she had kissed a man who was not her husband. And even before marrying, when she'd dated in high school, she'd had all of two boyfriends. Both of them short-term. So her kissing skills, while exercised and honed, had not been practiced on a variety of subjects. As well, those flirtation skills she might have once been proud of had not been utilized in any serious manner lately.

Last night's dive into the heady waters of pleasure had been delicious. Rez's mouth… She sighed to recall their kiss. And his hands moving over her body… So strong and holding her with such surety. She'd climbed onto his lap! No, she wasn't brazen. She'd just got lost in the moment, taking what she'd wanted.

Had he tugged open her shirt and glided his hand over her breasts she would have let it happen. Or would she? Who knew? She'd fled before it could go any further.

If he had been Brian she would have pushed him down and torn off his shirt. Because she'd been comfortable with her husband.

She wanted to do the same to Rez. She wanted…

What *did* she want to happen with Rez? Wild sex? Sure! But a relationship? Was she ready for all that *being a couple* entailed? What if something happened to him? She couldn't go through losing another man. Grief was not easy. And, much as she felt she had moved beyond it, she knew her heart was still fragile. Was it worth the risk of starting something with Rez when she couldn't know what that would bring?

"I'm not sure," she muttered aloud as she dropped a heavy leaf to the floor below. "Maybe I just need to let it happen. Right?"

Right. She was an adult. She could kiss a man if she wanted to. She could have sex with a man if she wanted to. Well, not on a first date. But she didn't need approval or permission from anyone. Not even her dead husband.

But she did need permission from herself.

"You have it," she told herself.

Now to really believe it.

It was six-thirty when Viv set aside the pruning shears for the day. The monstera had been removed from the ceiling and the wall. It had attached its aerial roots to the iron support frame, wedging itself between glass and metal. This species of plant was hardy, and determined, sometimes even attaching itself to smooth indoor walls to climb. Had it been cared for monthly it never would have grown of control. A small crack in one glass pane would have to be restored by a glazier, but there had been no damage to the metal frame.

Stepping back from the piles of cuttings she'd sorted, for disposal or repotting, she noticed her stomach growl. She hadn't even realized how hungry she was until now.

I need to head out for groceries.

Stopping in her room, she combed her shoulder-length hair and touched up her blush, then switched her tee shirt for a floral blouse. Back out in the foyer she met Rez, who was walking down the staircase. She hadn't realized he was home.

When he neared the bottom step he stumbled, and his palm slapped the newel post for support. Viv rushed over to him.

He thrust up a placating hand. "I missed the step," he said. "Wasn't paying attention."

"Oh." She ran her fingers up the back of her neck. The steps were wide, marble, and sturdy. Seemed pretty safe. And easily walkable. Hard to really miss a step because you weren't paying attention.

"I was distracted by a beautiful woman," he suddenly added.

"Oh?" Viv glanced around. "Where?"

She saw Rez's jaw fall open.

"Me?" Taking delight in her innocent ruse, she said, "I'd hate to be the reason for sending you head over heels."

"Really? Isn't that supposed to be a good thing?"

The subtle flirtation burned at the base of her neck.

"That it is," she said. "I was going out to find something for supper. Are you hungry?"

"I am, and we have the same goal. We can walk together."

"I'd like that. If you feel up for walking?"

"I am perfectly capable."

He gestured toward the door, where the coat rack held his suit jacket—and something she'd not noticed before. A cane.

"If you don't mind walking alongside a man with his cane?"

"If it helps you stay steady, I don't mind at all."

She followed him out the door and onto the sidewalk that led down the street to the smaller grocery and shops.

Noticing Rez glance around as if he were being watched, she said, "It's kind of sexy, actually. Your cane."

He chuckled. "You don't need to say that, Viv. I'm not an old man. This cane feels wrong. But I do need it."

"Of course you're not an old man. Nor am I an old woman."

"Far from it."

That statement was issued with a husky tone that swept her skin into a sensual awareness. "Then let's both agree not to worry about what others think. We are young, sexy, and—"

Rez glanced at her. "Did you call me sexy?"

"I did."

He looked ahead, but she caught the grin curling his mouth. "I'll take it."

Offering his free arm to hook with Viv's, he walked slowly. The cobbled street was punctuated with bollards at each end so no cars could drive it. The shops were old, cozy, and their displays invited browsing. But while Rez set the pace with a slow perusal of the shop windows, a needy impatience rose in Viv. She couldn't let things remain as they were.

"So," she said. "About last night."

How to tell him she was sorry about running off? But not sorry for kissing him. But in that moment she'd had to dash. Her crazy heart had reacted. A heart she'd thought had healed following her husband's death apparently still had a few cracks in it.

"I felt the same way." Rez turned his back to a display of chocolate bonbons. "About the kiss," he said.

"Yes, but—" Just what was *the same* to him?

"It was awesome."

"It was," she quickly said.

Whew! He hadn't felt she'd been awkward. Score one for the out-of-practice kisser.

"But you rushing off like that…"

Oh, no, here it comes.

"You needed to do that," he said. "And, honestly, I needed that distance myself. *Oui?*"

"*Oui.* It wasn't because I didn't like the kiss, or us, or—"

"I know," he said. "No need to explain. Or apologize. And, so you know, I'd like to kiss you again. Whenever you want it to happen."

"Oh. Well."

Yes! Every nerve ending in Viv's body suddenly glittered. Her inner bouncy teenager surfaced.

"I feel the same. I…uh… Well, it's my silly heart."

"Your heart is silly?"

"It is when I think I've come to terms with something but it decides I have not. This is new to me, Rez. I mean, being intimate with someone who isn't—"

She didn't want to bring her husband into this conversation. She didn't need Brian's memory as a shield. Did she?

"Same," Rez said. He held out his hand to her. "Let's see what happens."

Viv put her hand in his. The invitation felt immense and open to so much. "I'm all in."

CHAPTER SEVEN

REZ SUGGESTED THEY eat in a restaurant so Viviane wouldn't have to cook. Not that she *had* to cook, he quickly added.

"I love to cook. But I won't refuse a dinner date." She squeezed his hand. "Can we call this a date? It would be my first in decades. What about you? Have you dated since—well...?"

He sensed she was nervous. He felt those fluttery wings in his gut as well. One thing he'd learned since his wife's passing: people never knew how to speak about his loss. Awkward questions abounded. And that sad look of forced concern was growing tired. Yet he was comfortable with Viv, because she understood and had probably experienced much the same.

"I have tried to date," he said as they walked. "Twice, actually. Never made it to that first kiss, though. Didn't feel right to me."

"Yes, it's weird. I mean, our actual kiss wasn't weird. It's the getting close to a new person part of it that's sort of...you know...weird."

"Exactly. And you are not weird."

"Just strange?"

He laughed. "A little. So… It's a date."

Her cheeks pinkened. Simplicity and ease, this woman. Completely the opposite of Colette, who had been high maintenance. Maintenance he had not minded.

Rez had lavished his wife with clothing, shoes, jewels—anything she'd wanted. He couldn't imagine Viv being comfortable in a crystal-laden ball gown or walking in stilettos. The dark pants and slightly rumpled blouse suited her. And he wouldn't tell her about the dirt smudge on her knee.

He veered them toward his favorite restaurant, a four-star establishment that required reservations months in advance. He'd yet to need one. The owner's wife had an account with Le Beau and used it often.

He gestured toward the front door, where the liveried hostess checked her iPad and spoke to guests, and as he did so he felt Viv's resistance in her tug at their clasped hands.

"What is it?"

"This place looks a little too fancy for how I'm dressed," she said. "I don't know…"

"You look lovely. They don't judge attire here, only taste."

"But it looks busy."

"I'm sure it is. Come along, *ma chérie*. You've been walking every morning, talking to ducks, taking in Paris from the ground level. Now I want you to see my city from a different perspective."

With a nervous tug to her lower lip with her teeth—she did that often, and it gave him shivers...the good kind—she nodded and allowed him to lead her onward.

The hostess, with impeccable make-up and sleek black hair, smiled as Rez approached. "Monsieur Ricard! Your usual table?"

"Oui, merci."

She spun around the podium and smiled warmly at Viv, which Rez appreciated. Viv noticeably relaxed as she followed the hostess. Rez took up behind her, his cane still supporting his steps. That Viv hadn't blinked at his using it made it a little less humiliating.

Traversing the curling steel staircase upward, they landed in the roof dining area. Only three tables up here. Hundreds of potted plants framed the rooftop, forming a thick hedge but not blocking the view of the city. Sparkling fairy lights were strung across the laticed canopy. And a soft tango sounded through speakers hidden within the foliage.

"Champagne?" the hostess asked as she showed them to the farthest table, which was canopied by climbing greenery.

"Let's start with wine," he said. "Whatever the sommelier recommends."

The hostess left them. Viviane ran her fingers

across a frothy plant that Rez thought might be a fern, but really he had no clue. Sounds of marvel gasped from her lips as she found her way to the stone balustrade at the corner of the roof. On tiptoes, she took in the view, panning the cityscape.

"Amazing, isn't it?" Rez walked up behind her.

"This is incredible. There's the Eiffel Tower. And I can see the Ferris wheel in the Tuileries. And over there is the Arc du Triomphe! Wow. When you said you wanted to give me a different perspective of the city you weren't kidding. And…" she turned and took in the rooftop "…we're the only ones up here. Just how rich do you have to be to be able to sashay in like we did?"

"Very." He pulled out a chair for her before the table. "I hope you don't mind a surprise meal. It's chef's choice when you're seated up here. I've never been disappointed."

The sommelier arrived with wine. They exchanged a quick conversation in French about the engagement ring Rez had designed for his son's fiancée. And then, after he'd tasted the Bordeaux and assured the man it was plush and darkly sweet, they were again left alone.

Viv sipped the wine. Her eyes brightened. "This is… I don't even have words for this wine. It tastes like…plums?"

"It's from near the Gironde estuary. Their terroir is impeccable. It's a bit sweet, but smooth."

"I love sweet wine. Well, I just love wine. But not too much. I'm not a lush."

With a nervous laugh, she looked at the lights strung across the rooftop. Rez noticed the freckles dancing across her nose and cheeks. More proof she was indeed a garden nymph.

"It's like a fantasy world up here," she said.

"I'm glad you like it. I haven't been here in years. I'm surprised they even remember me."

"I suspect the owner of Le Beau is difficult to forget. And you are handsome. Remarkable."

"Says the prettiest woman in the place."

Her laughter was forced, but he suspected the blush was not. He really did enjoy her blushes.

"I'll take that. It's been a while since I've felt pretty."

"Why?" He leaned forward. "You are a natural beauty. I imagine you tumble from bed and you're ready to go."

She shrugged. "You don't want to hear my beauty routine. But it's nice to get a compliment. To tell you the truth…" She toyed with the silverware, her mood growing more solemn. "I've thought about such things since my husband's death. After being married for so long, we often forget to tell our loved one simple things, like *You are handsome* or *You make me happy.* Am I right?"

He nodded. He didn't want the conversation to turn to their lost loves. He wasn't sure he could talk about Colette so casually with another woman.

Yet. But she was right. He'd complimented Colette often. Yet had she ever called him handsome, as Viv just had? Made him feel…worthy? That was an odd thing to realize. His bank account proved his worth was billions. His reputation was impeccable. But to be admired by someone like Viv, who seemed so genuine and open, superseded that material status.

"I'm sorry. I forget that not everyone is on the same acceptance level with their grief as I am. We don't have to talk about our spouses," she offered. "I'm still learning how to be this thing called 'widow.'" She made a face, nose scrunched. "Being referred to as a widow feels so dismissive. And it's always accompanied by a sad moue. Yes, I lost my husband. But you know…life goes on. I didn't crumble and you don't have to treat me with kid gloves."

"Kid gloves?"

"It's a way of saying to take excessive care or concern with someone. I'm sure you must have gotten the same treatment."

"I did, and still do. But do you have children? How have they managed the loss?"

"We never had kids. Both of us loved them, but not so much that we wanted to grow our family. Brian and I enjoyed working together and that was what worked best for us. How is your son with his mom's absence?"

"It is difficult for Jean-Louis. He and his mother were close. He…"

It had been Jean-Louis who had stepped in for Rez when he'd been recuperating in the hospital after the accident. His son had handled the reins of Le Beau without issues. At a time when he should have focused on his grief.

"My son has lost a lot. Sometimes I forget that I'm not the only one affected by my wife's death. I agree with you. We've survived a painful experience and we're still here. On to the next adventure?"

"You don't sound so sure about that."

She'd guessed exactly right. There were days when he was ready to dash forward and begin a whole new chapter. Other days he wanted to reread his favorite parts and cling to those memories. And why hadn't he talked to Jean-Louis about his grief? Le Beau was their common interest; they'd never been close beyond that.

But he couldn't pull the mopey act now. Because Viviane intrigued him. And whatever was happening between the two of them… He wanted it to happen.

"What's more sure than sitting across the table from a beautiful woman on a date?"

She beamed at him. "If it is an official date, that means I'll get another kiss out of the deal."

"Of course you will."

But just as he considered leaning over to kiss

her, the waiter arrived with their first course. And a new wine.

"How do you like the red?" Rez asked, after Viviane had tried it.

"It's quite special. You do love your wine. Is that a French thing?"

"Could be. And I own a vineyard."

"Wow. Where is it?"

"In the Rhône Valley. It's southeast of Paris. If you'd like a tour, I'd be happy to take you there."

"Really? I would like that. I usually take the weekends off. Unless you want me to work. You are the boss."

"That I am," he said, and the second course was served.

After cheese, salads, a tiny concoction of lamb and what had been described as an onion mousse, the dessert plate was delivered. Four small *bon-bons* gleamed under the fairy lights. Viv cut one in half on her plate and cooed at the layered filling.

She was not self-aware, he thought, and would laugh without a care. And those freckles highlighted by the golden glow... They fascinated him. He must make a freckle count on her soon. She was so easy to be with. Rez wanted to learn all he could about her.

"What was the last good book you read?" he asked.

"Really? You want to know what I read?"

"Of course. I read all the time. I prefer adventure fantasy stuff, like Jim Butcher."

Viv almost choked on her bite of dessert. "Seriously? You like Butcher? I love the Harry Dresden series. Bob is my favorite."

"A talking skull? You have to love that."

Viv sighed. "Wow. You just got infinitely sexier."

Rez quirked a brow. "I thought I was already sexy?"

"Oh, yes. But you got more sexy." She dramatically fanned her face. "Whew! Give me the lift of a brow any day and I'm happy."

Rez laughed. "If that's all you want, then you're easy."

"Oh, men!" Viv declared dramatically. "I'm never easy. My material wants are few, but my emotional wants are great."

"Let me guess. Companionship, trust, and love?"

"I'm impressed. You got it on the first try."

"I think everyone wants those things, Viv."

"Especially people who have loved and lost?"

Rez slid his hand across the table to touch hers. Because he couldn't *not* make such a move. She compelled him.

"Even us," Rez said. "We're not different from anyone else walking the streets, are we?"

"Most definitely not. Though I will confess that knowledge struck me hard a few months after Brian died."

"How so?"

"I was in a store one day, randomly wandering the aisles. I'd just spent five minutes in the car, bawling over an AC/DC song. That was his favorite band. I only heard that song at specific times following his death. It was him speaking to me—I know it."

"I can understand that." He'd not had any signs from Colette—not that he had noticed—but he could relate to specific things dredging up memories. Like roses…

"Anyway, I wiped the tears away and went inside to find some cereal and fruit. I saw a child crying, and his mother muttered to me that he'd lost his dog earlier that morning. I know now that it doesn't matter if you've lost a dog, a friend, or a spouse of decades. You can't know what the person standing in line next to you is going through. If they're happy. If they've lost someone. Grief is universal. We have to learn to move with it. Take it as life gives it to you. And for some reason that allowed me to rise up from the tearful days and move onward."

"No more tears at all?"

"Oh, dear… I cry at everything. Especially movies. But I don't cry when I hear AC/DC now, because I take a moment to remember. And those memories make me happy."

Rez clasped his hands before his face, blowing out a breath. He wished his memories were the same. But the accident had changed his memory. Made it difficult to keep hold of some things. Obliterated other memories. He sensed some memories about Colette had been stolen, because when he thought about their marriage, their life together, there were spaces—blocks he couldn't recall. Had they been a happy couple? Most of the time... Colette had been a model. He had been the husband standing in her shadow, little bothered by the shade. But there had been times he'd wondered if he was making her happy. On an emotional level.

Well, it didn't matter anymore, did it?

"You have memories?" she asked.

"I do. And I don't. The accident knocked my brain hard. It's called traumatic brain injury. I have trouble with short-term stuff, like appointments and what I went into the kitchen to look for. But, as well, I can't remember anything about the night of the accident. Only a feeling of terror as the car swerved off the road. And then I woke in the hospital and was told my wife was dead."

Viviane threaded her fingers through his. "I can't imagine losing a spouse in an instant like that. At the very least I had three years to say goodbye as Brian struggled with cancer. You woke to a life without your wife. I'm sorry."

"Thank you," he whispered. "I...don't talk about this with anyone."

"I don't want to intrude on your grief," she said.

"You're not. Being with you…another soul who has been through what I have…makes it easier. I won't make the mistake of calling you easy again, but you are…comfortable to be around, Viv."

And then he found his moment. The tableware might glisten like gold in the city lights, but it was Viv's face that truly blossomed in this golden moment.

"Six," he said.

"What?"

"Six freckles on that cheek. And on the other…" He bowed his head to make a count. "Six. If there are six on your nose…"

"No one has ever done a freckle-count on me before. I warn you, I have some on my shoulders. A lot."

"Six on your nose," he announced. "And I look forward to exploring your shoulders."

She gave his hand a squeeze. "Is it all right if we sit here for a bit?"

The city breathed around them. The night air was perfumed with flowers, softening Rez's anxiety over his missing memories. And Viv's presence coaxed him away from dire thoughts. She was so fascinating in her quirky manner, and a little strange. Talking to cats and crystals…? He smirked.

"What?"

"I was just wondering what sort of stone you have in your bra this evening."

Viv laughed. "It's the moonstone."

"Can I see it?"

She looked to each side. No people on the roof besides them. She tucked her finger under her neckline and mined the stone from her bra. It flashed under the hanging lights. She handed it to him.

"It's warm."

"It was just tucked against the girls."

He snickered. He wouldn't mind being tucked in the same spot.

He held up the stone and studied the flash. "That's called chatoyancy, the flash."

"Really? Cool. I love the piece. I've been carrying it with me every day since I've been in Paris."

"Doesn't it ever...fall out?"

"Sometimes I do forget I've tucked a crystal in there, and when I get undressed at night it'll fall to the floor. Broke a perfectly good fluorite once."

"You know, there is an easier way to keep a precious stone close. Can I set this for you?"

"Oh. Well, I'd love that, but I'm sure I can't afford your work."

"Nonsense." Rez shook the stone on his palm. "Consider it part of the payment for your work. A bonus. *Oui?*"

She nodded.

He tucked the moonstone in a pocket. "Let's walk."

CHAPTER EIGHT

REZ SCROLLED TO Coral's number in his phone. His finger hovered over "call." His brows furrowed. The cup of morning coffee sitting on the kitchen counter steamed near his hip. From the hallway, he heard footsteps approaching the kitchen.

Quickly, he tried to summon one reason why he needed to expel Viviane from his home. While the usual argument was obvious, it didn't rise as necessarily urgent. Her work in the garden had saved him from a disaster. The whole ceiling could have been pulled down from the weight of the overgrown foliage. A touch-up on the conservatory would also increase the sale price on the mansion.

And, if he was honest, he enjoyed Viviane's company. And counting her freckles. And kissing her. He reached into his trouser pocket and pulled out the moonstone cabochon. Nestled against her breasts all day? What a place to be.

"Good morning. Or is that *bonjour*?"

She wandered into the bright sunlight. Hair gathered into a messy chignon and leather garden gloves on, she clasped her hands before her and waited for him to reply.

Rez was still lost in the sparkle of her eyes. The utter freshness of her standing next to him. It was as if she carried in new air along with her. He inhaled, gathering as much of her as he could. Green, vibrant, airy.

"Rez?"

"*Bonjour?* You've got it correct," he said. "Though I think the spunkier *salut* might fit you as well."

"You think I'm spunky?"

"You project a certain bouncy appeal."

"I can do bouncy." She waggled her shoulders in example.

Rez slid a finger over the home screen, then tucked the phone inside his suit pocket. Coral could wait.

"There's coffee."

"I can smell that. How's the leg feeling this morning?"

"Tight, but Henri is waiting outside for me. I see you've already dug into the garden?"

She splayed a gloved hand. "Just bagging up the last of the debris. According to a schedule I found in the supply room, garbage pick-up is this afternoon, so I want to get that out."

"I can help you." He'd seen five or six large paper bags filled with foliage nestled by the back door. "Before I leave."

"Are you sure?" She slid a glance down to his leg.

Rez straightened, taking offense at the unspoken cut. It was emasculating enough having to use the cane on occasion. "I'm not feeble."

"I know you're not."

But did she?

"Let's do it now so Henri isn't kept too long."

He headed for the refuse bags. When the final bag had been hauled out, Rez leaned against the limestone wall that backed up his property. Viv had carried out two bags to his four.

"I appreciate the help," she said, swiping aside a strand of hair from her face. "Gardening is a lot of heavy lifting. I can manage this particular job on my own, but I'll have to hire local muscle on future jobs. You available?"

Rez chuckled. "If it's in Paris, sure."

He reached to wipe a dirt smudge from her forehead. It was stubborn. He licked his thumb, but when he got close to her face she dodged.

"Is that a mother thing?" she asked.

He looked at his thumb. "I suppose… Sorry."

"It's okay." She laughed, and crossed her eyes in an attempt to look up at her forehead.

Mon Dieu, did he love her laughter.

When she licked her own thumb and tried to swipe at the smudge, he clasped her wrist to direct her to the right spot. That sheen of dirt was stubborn; he decided he'd let her get it all later. But he didn't drop her hand.

"Is it gone?" she asked.

"Most of it. I like you rumpled."

"You…*like* me?"

He made show of wobbling his head, as if giving it some thought, but really he could have answered much faster. "I've decided I enjoy having some 'strange' in my life. You've grown on me—much like that crazy plant you took down in the conservatory."

"That plant almost cost you a big repair bill."

"The money doesn't matter."

"I suppose not."

The next seconds were silent as their gazes spoke more loudly than words. Hope and kindness beamed in Viviane's green eyes. He wondered if she could see the need to trust in his. He had been hurt emotionally, but in ways he still struggled to pinpoint.

"I suppose Henri is wondering what's taking you so long," she prompted.

He'd forgotten about his waiting driver. And about the fact that he did have a job which required him to leave this house, this woman.

This woman. She had altered his perspective in ways he wasn't even aware of. He just knew he liked what Viviane did to him.

He nodded, but still he held her hand. "Now that you've finished that project, you may go ahead with the refurbishment in the rest of the garden. With the exception of the roses on the north side."

Her jaw dropped open.

"I still can't make contact with Coral," he lied. "And now that I've seen what you can do, I know sprucing up the conservatory will be worthwhile."

"Oh, I can do that! Thank you, Rez—er... Monsieur Ricard."

Not liking being addressed by her that way, Rez reacted. He bent to kiss her. Quickly. But their lips connected as if designed for one another. They knew their place, marked it, and then parted.

"It's Rez," he said, and pressed his forehead to hers. "I think we've moved beyond formalities."

"Rez. But...uh...you *are* officially my employer. Do the French always kiss the hired help?"

"Not always." Rez stood back and adjusted his tie. He winked at her and decided that a parting smile was all she required as explanation for that.

"If you tell me when you'll be home," she called as he strolled away, "I'll have a meal ready."

"Early," he decided, even as his brain told him that was very un-Rez-like. "Five."

"I'll see you then!"

As he headed toward the foyer an irrepressible smile curled his mouth. He even ignored the cane hanging on the coat rack as he exited the mansion.

Viviane lay on the tiled conservatory floor. She had won over the staunch owner! In more ways than one. What an interesting way of advancing her employment. Smooching the owner. She wondered what he would do if she slept with him?

"Never say never," she said with a smile.

The room's humidity was rising. She'd adjusted the temperature controls that morning. Now she could look to salvaging the entire garden. There was much to do, according to the plan she'd detailed in her notebook. Today she would work on the lower vegetation. It all needed trimming and new mulch around the roots. A soft moss base would be perfect. As for those ratty white wicker chairs set in the back circle of the room…

They would go. And in their place? Something elegant, but cozy. A place where a person could relax and forget the world. Stretch out, curl up with a fantasy book.

She pushed her fingers through her hair, closing her eyes to the bright sunlight that beamed through the glass roof. Lying here, in a multi-million-dollar mansion—in Paris—was beyond fantasy. It was incredible. An amazing gift. And she did not take it lightly. Top it off with a handsome millionaire who had actually showed interest in her, and who was an incredible kisser, and she might be walking in a dream. Was she sleeping?

She snapped a finger against her temple. *Ouch.* This was not a dream.

Despite the fact that she had come to terms with being single, and now actually enjoyed it, she did crave companionship, sharing conversation…

The connection. Heck, touching another human body....

Yes, she wanted to have sex with Rez. Was she ready to make that dive? She had been married for twenty-five years. Including college boyfriends, she'd only ever had three sexual partners. And one had been a constant for two and a half decades. Could she really open herself to intimacy with a new man?

"Yes," she whispered aloud.

But it felt daunting. When they were married, a person got used to routine. It hadn't been a big thing to undress before her husband, to walk around in holey underwear, to be seen tugging her bra out from her shirtsleeve after a long day at work. Heck, even to fart in his presence. And to admit to all the things that should never be spoken out loud.

Rez was... Well, he was the homecoming king who made her feel giddy and blush whenever he looked her way. And she knew they were not hot flashes. How to go beyond kisses with him? Did *he* want that? She'd not forgotten how to have sex—had she? Maybe. No! It was a natural thing. Just like kissing. New partners always provoked nervousness and a lack of confidence. Right?

Viv blew out a breath. She was overthinking this. If sex was on the table, she'd go with it. But she sensed that until Rez completely trusted her they would never get past making out, as they had briefly following their meal in the restaurant last night. A kiss goodnight once they'd walked inside the mansion. Oh, so lovely. But he still grieved his wife. And Viv didn't want to push him. He might grieve for Colette the rest of his life. Never incorporate that grief into his life in a manner which didn't prevent new relationships from blossoming.

The thought of Brian sometimes made Viv smile, sometimes cry. Some days she didn't think of him at all. Other days, seeing a perfectly round boxwood shrub could reduce her to tears. But she was coping. And she did not feel she was cheating on Brian with Rez. She had a right to move forward.

Rolling onto her stomach, she propped her chin on her fists and eyed the thorny rose bushes. This project could not be a success unless she was granted permission to prune them. If they had been his wife's favorites then he should *want* them tamed, able to grow and provide him with wonderful memories year after year. All Viv had to do was trim them way back and…

Ah, heck.

She finally got it.

Tonight's meal was a mix of charcuterie and cheeses, along with crispy baguettes and macarons. Viviane had gathered the spread during her afternoon walk. The wine was sweet, the cheese remarkable, and the man across the table from her was gorgeous. But she'd been troubled since figuring out those rose bushes earlier. And she'd never been adept at ignoring her curiosity.

With a long sip of wine to fortify her courage, Viv said, "I'm sorry, Rez. I finally understand about the roses. The whole garden. You think I'm destroying your wife's memory."

The man set down his baguette slice and rubbed his palms along his thighs. She thought the look he gave her said a lot. *Oh, you...the American woman who likes to constantly challenge me. Not giving me a moment to enjoy this meal?*

Ready to apologize for her apology, Viv lifted her chin—and then silenced that worry. They were adults. They could talk about the tough stuff. They had last night at the restaurant.

"It's not that you're destroying her memory," Rez said. "The garden is *my* memory."

"I get that. And the more I rearrange and trim in the garden the more I tramp on the things your wife cherished. I get it, Rez. And I'm so sorry I didn't make the connection sooner. If I touch those roses, I'm touching something only your wife touched. I'm changing them. And then your memory is changed."

He pushed back on his chair, head bowed. Viv could feel his anger—no, it wasn't that. It was... sorrow?

"I don't want to step on her memory," Viv said

softly. "And I know you're tired of me arguing about this with you, but please hear me out."

Crossing his arms, he kept his head bowed. A partial agreement to listen. That was better than him storming out.

"Those roses were once beautiful. Perhaps they remind you of your wife's beauty. But they've gone wild and are in desperate need of pruning. I'm surprised they haven't died." She swallowed. Not the best word-choice, but she had to be honest. "They won't survive much longer. But if you'll allow me to trim them back—and I warn you, it would be extreme, leaving them as stubs for the rest of this growing season—then I promise the results will be stunning. And I don't wish to make any presumptions on behalf of..." she winced "...her..."

"Then don't," he said roughly.

"But, Rez, I think if your wife loved those roses she would be utterly torn to see them in the condition they are now. She would want them restored. Flourishing."

"You're right," he said, and stood abruptly, plucking the wine bottle from the table. "You shouldn't presume anything."

With that, he marched out of the kitchen.

Viv leaned over the table and caught her forehead in hand. She'd had to try...

CHAPTER NINE

THE NEXT EVENING, Henri pulled the limo up before the mansion. Sitting in the back, Rez felt his thoughts turn toward the woman in his conservatory.

Colette's conservatory.

His wife had been thrilled to find the mansion up for sale only months after they'd married. She'd attended a wild party there in her teens, and had told him about the garden in which she'd gotten high with her friends. Her desire to own that garden had been enough for him to gift the mansion to her as a belated wedding present.

Colette had spent the weekend there perhaps once a month during the early years of their marriage. Then, as her modeling career had fizzled in her late thirties, her stays had grown more frequent. Her time had been spent gardening and painting. She had asked Rez visit only with her invitation. It had been her private lair…an escape from the Parisian bustle.

He'd been fine with that request. Colette had been a particular woman; he'd catered to her needs.

Besides, his design work had always kept him busy. There had been many days when he'd only seen his wife as he'd arrived home to kiss her goodnight. They'd grown distant in later years. Yes, he could have set his own work schedule and given Colette more of his time. But he had not. And the reason for it niggled at his faulty memory.

Had they fallen out of love?

He had to stop mulling over a woman he could never resurrect. He didn't need Colette back in his life. Cruel as the accident had been, he understood that death was final, and it happened every day—to so many. Yet Viv had been right about the reason why he'd not wanted her to touch the roses. She'd also been right that preserving them would have been what Colette most wanted.

Overall…? He was putting too much energy into fighting what wasn't a battle at all.

"*Merci*, Henri."

He got out of the limo and strolled up the walk to the house.

Time to be an adult.

Rez walked through the front door to find a green velvet sofa sitting in the foyer. On the couch sat a gorgeous woman in chinos and a tee shirt, one arm across the back of the settee, the other hand holding a goblet of wine. A wine bottle and another goblet sat on the floor by her feet.

"What is this?"

"Coral approved me purchasing new furniture

for the garden. It was part of my contract. But I suppose I should have asked you… I'm sorry."

"Not to worry. I honor the contract you have with Coral. But why is it in the foyer and not in the conservatory?"

"The one delivery man who could speak a meager amount of English insisted they had not been paid to place the couch. Only to get it in the front door. I offered him more money and he tutted at me and said it was lunchtime." She swallowed a gulp of wine. Shrugged. "You could use some furniture out here, I suppose…"

Rez chuckled and sat next to her. He poured himself a glass, and then kissed her cheek. "You like to make lemon cake with lemons?"

"I think you're going for lemonade with that one."

Rez bounced on the cushions. "Comfy. Very big."

"And heavy," she said. "I can't even lift an end without worrying about hurting my back. I was going to call a furniture mover, but I've gone beyond my patience with the free translation app on my phone. And Harley, who can speak French, is incommunicado. Would you mind calling for me?"

"Those movers should have taken it into the garden. I will have words with them."

"I like that. Forceful. Manly." She gave his biceps a squeeze. "So…you're home early?"

"Yes, and I want to talk to you about last night."

"Oh?"

"I'm sorry. I shouldn't have walked out on our conversation like that."

"Apologies are not necessary. I understand. I've no right to tell you what your wife may or may not have approved."

"No, you don't. And I still wish the roses to remain untouched. For now. Let me sit on it a few more days and then we'll see if I change my mind."

She clasped his hand. "You can take all the time you need. I've enough work with the rest of the garden right now. And I promise I am taking great care with all of it."

"I know that you are." He turned to face her.

"So you're not mad at me?"

"I find it impossible to remain angry with the strange and beautiful nymph who lives in my garden."

Her eyebrow lifted. "Go on."

"I desire you, Viviane. And, while I don't feel like it's cheating on a dead woman, it's something new for me. I trust you. You understand what I'm going through. Impossible to believe that you can be here, right now, when I need someone like you the most."

"Do you believe in fate? Destiny? Soul mates?"

"Never given it much thought."

"Well, I have, and I've never believed in soul mates. I believe that people can love more than one person romantically in their lifetime. One person does not have to be your *one*."

"I'm with you on that."

Because he'd never felt Colette had been his soul mate—rather his wife, his lover. Friends, of course. However, there had been something about their relationship… It was so frustrating that he could not remember! The truth about him and Colette had been torn from his memory the night of the accident.

Viv stretched out a leg and tilted back her head. Her sleek body teased him. Gorgeous, relaxed, luscious in its simpleness.

He wasn't sure what he wanted to happen right now. Talking? Kissing? Sex? Still felt too soon for that. But not for touch and connection. Feeling Viv's body heat against his aroused him. He was so ready to kiss this woman.

"Eighteen freckles," he whispered as he moved to kiss the tip of her nose, then each of her cheeks. "You make me feel eighteen again, Viv."

She set down her goblet and then performed a slide of her leg along his hip and thigh that directed him to follow her. They landed horizontally on the spacious sofa. And his long-lost teenager knew exactly what to do.

"I haven't made out on a couch in forever," she said as he kissed along her jaw and down her neck. "Mmm… I like that."

Anything she liked he was eager to continue.

Licking her soft skin, he devoured the vibrant greenness, the nymph's alluring perfume. The feel of her breasts under his palms made him rock-hard. The undulation of her body beneath his coaxed him in for a deeper kiss. He wanted to fall into her. Get lost.

And yet she gently broke the kiss and bracketed his face with her hands. "I'm not quite ready for...you know..."

"Do I know?"

"Sex..."

Rez snickered. "Are you asking me or telling me?"

"Telling *and* asking?"

He nodded. "I'm not ready, either. But I want you, Viv."

"You do?"

"I'm distracted by thoughts of you at work."

"I like being a distraction. Kiss me again. And whatever you do...don't move your hands."

His hands which were on her breasts? He did appreciate a woman who knew what she wanted.

The garden was coming along nicely. And that was amazing, considering she was doing it all by herself. With encouragement from Harley. Her social media was attracting followers. The Plant Whisperer logo Harley had created featured a vector image of a pair of pink pursed lips next to a plant. It was sexy and cute at the same time.

Harley had also reported a sudden uptick in her book sales. So word was getting out.

The moving team had arrived first thing this morning, and now the green velvet sofa sat at the back of the conservatory in the round gathering area. Oh, that sofa… Viv could not think of it as anything but the make-out sofa now. What a way to break in new furniture!

Unable to find a tarp or any plastic to protect it from dirt, she had tossed the extra blanket she'd found in her closet over it. It would serve as protection until she was done with the dirt-flinging process.

Now, sitting on the floor before the sofa, she worked on her business plan over a light lunch of a ham and goat cheese croissant and the Orangina she had come to love, despite its sugar content.

She could afford an assistant—probably hired hourly at each location she worked at rather than salaried, because then she'd have to pay travel expenses—and still bring in a profit. The more jobs she completed, the better her resume would look and the more she could charge. Then there was the issue of supplies. She'd had to purchase a set of clippers, and would always need pots, dirt, wiring, mulch, et cetera. The supply room here had three-quarters of the things she required, but future jobs might not have anything.

The landscaping business she and Brian had built together had been considered elite, and they'd serviced million-dollar homes in the Minneapolis suburbs. Together, they had garnered awards and honors for their work. Now it was simply a matter of rebuilding a client base. In Europe. It would be a lot of hard work and would rely on word of mouth. And excellent marketing. She loved a challenge.

Viv set aside the business plan and leaned back on her palms. The tessellated tile floor in the conservatory featured indigo, moss, and cream colors, with an iridescent tile fitted in here and there to provide a startling gleam. She went and sat beneath a fern she'd trimmed to half its original width and height. It was still almost four feet tall, and though it had been less than a week since its trim it had already straightened and unfurled.

Straight and unfurled… That was how she felt when she was with Rez. Her shoulders lifted, her neck straightened—everything inside her that had curled and withered following Brian's death began to reach out, open, and seek. It was an empowering feeling.

When taking this offer in Paris she'd counted on a path to a new job. But romance…?

"The sun on your face makes you beam like a golden idol."

Startled by Rez's voice, Viv looked up. Clad in what she could only guess was a designer business suit worth a few mortgage payments, he also wore a black shirt and tie beneath the deep blue coat, which granted him a stylish, elegant figure. He exuded calm confidence. And so much sex appeal.

"You're home early," she said.

Had that sounded like a spouse complaining? Old habits and all that jazz?

"I've a quick trip to Versailles this afternoon. Henri picks me up in ten minutes."

"How can a trip to Versailles ever be quick? That place is amazing."

"So you've been there?"

"Not yet. I've only seen photos of it in books. But I hope to work it in as a weekend trip."

"If I didn't have this meeting I'd take you along. Perhaps soon, though?"

"I'd like that. So, what sort of business does a jeweler have at Versailles?"

"Le Beau will be part of a Christmas exhibit that will feature the royal jewels and other Parisian designers. I want to create a new piece, so a consultation with the exhibit planners is necessary. It'll be donated for a charitable cause."

"That's generous. You really love designing jewelry," she said, knowing it was true.

"It is a passion."

"Did you ever design anything for your wife?"

"Many pieces. She favored black diamonds." He smiled as he shoved his hands in his front pockets. "I must admit, until I met you, I would dodge any questions or conversations regarding my wife. But you make it seem not so dreadful to summon her memory."

"I'll take that as a good thing. Memory can be a wondrous way to heal the soul. So you'll be home late?"

Again, did she sound like a spouse?

Watch it, Viv, you're not the man's keeper. Or his wife.

But did she want to be?

Nah. Not...yet.

"After dinner, for sure. Please don't wait up for me."

"I won't. I intend to walk this evening. Take in the city lights."

"Be sure to visit the Fifth. It's an interesting assortment of entertainment at night. There's tango dancing down by the river."

"Really? I prefer slow dances. I want to peek into Notre Dame as well. See how the reconstruction looks and if they're holding services."

"Sounds like you have the evening planned. I...uh... I have a question for you."

"Shoot."

"Would you be interested in going to a lavish party with me this Saturday?"

That was three days away. She had nothing to wear. And she could imagine how lavish it would be, especially knowing the set that Rez ran with.

"Hmm…"

"Don't refuse. Please. It's Le Beau's one-hundredth anniversary celebration. Jean-Louis has planned the entire thing. It'll be my chance to show him and all our clients that I am still capable and not a fumbling idiot who needs to be put out to pasture."

"Well, you don't need me to prove that."

"But I want you at my side."

If it was possible to unfurl even more, Viviane did so. But could she pull it off? Standing on the arm of a millionaire and convincing others that he considered her as a potential date?

"I'll take your silence as agreement," he teased.

"Rez, it's not that I don't love spending time with you. But I'm not sure I can do the fancy ball thing. I've only packed work clothes, and—"

"Oh, I'm taking you shopping. That's part of the date."

"It is?" She wrinkled a brow.

"Yes. A fancy gown is necessary. Shoes… And if you want your hair and make-up done I'll make it happen. Let me treat you."

"A gown, eh? *And* a date for the ball?"

"I'm not sure it's a ball. More of a standing around and schmoozing while we look at pretty jewels event. A *soirée*."

"But it is a celebration of your company. You must be very proud."

"I am." Rez's phone buzzed in his pocket. "That's Henri."

He bowed to kiss her forehead and Viv reached up to pull him down for a better kiss.

"Yes, I'll be your date."

CHAPTER TEN

COLETTE HAD NEVER invited Rez along on her frequent and hours-long excursions to the high-end stores dotting the Rue de Rivoli and the Champs-Élysées. And, frankly, following a woman from store to store, sitting on the sidelines while she tried on clothes, shoes, intimates, whatever, did not make his list of top ways to spend an afternoon.

On the other hand, he did enjoy taking a woman shopping for jewelry. *His* jewelry. It was all about designing the perfect piece for a woman.

He hadn't the leisure to design anything for Viv to wear this weekend—the moonstone she'd trusted him with wasn't set—but he did want to see her in some sparkles for the event. He wouldn't know what to put on her until he'd seen what she'd be wearing.

While he guessed she wouldn't be able to afford anything they would be looking at today, it pleased him to be able to treat her. Not because he wanted to woo her with expensive gifts. She wasn't a woman impressed by material things. No, he simply wanted to see her happy. Smiling. And, of course, wearing something appropriate for an event that would be filled with old money, celebrities, and a few royals.

One shop he knew that carried suitable gowns sat on the Avenue Montaigne, which Colette had frequented. He knew that because he'd gotten the bills. When he walked into the shop with Viv on his arm he got a raised eyebrow from the woman behind the counter. He suspected she knew who he was, and most certainly had known his wife.

"Monsieur Ricard."

The clerk smiled politely, and then inquired as to what he needed. Stepping back and allowing Viv to explain what she liked, including colors and styles, Rez was directed to the waiting area in a private salon.

With a tumbler of surprisingly smooth whiskey in hand, and a silver tray of pastries at his side, Rez stretched his free arm across the back of a red velvet divan and studied the chandelier. De Clerc, if he were not mistaken. He and the De Clerc family had known one another for decades. Their kids had gone to the same schools, and often vacationed together. Jean-Louis had even dated one of the De Clerc daughters for a few months one summer.

Rez enjoyed taking vacations, but he couldn't recall when he'd last done so. For he and Colette's honeymoon? Surely they'd gone elsewhere since that trip to St. Barth's? Had it been him or Colette who had been too busy to coordinate schedules? Possibly him. Workaholic was a label he embraced.

Hell. Had he been to blame for their waning emotions toward one another? Should he have tried harder? Been there for Colette.

He had been. He really had been.

So why did he feel as if he'd done something wrong?

Viv peeked out from the dressing room for the third time, dispelling his self-effacing thoughts. The first two times she'd worn a frown. Red was too bold for her, distracting from her gleaming copper-blonde hair. And white was too difficult—or that was how she'd explained it.

"Even though I've never liked the color, I think this is the one," she said now. She popped out of the room, landing on her tiptoes, arms extended. "Ta-da!"

Rez leaned forward, whiskey forgotten. She smoothed her hands down the violet lace from waist to thigh, then twirled slowly to show off the long, body-hugging gown. The bodice glinted with tiny crystals set in a damask pattern that curled and spiraled up to sheer sleeves with even finer glints. It accentuated her long, graceful neck. It revealed the tops of her luscious yet small breasts. And it did something wonderful to her overall.

Did she stand a little taller? Did her chin lift

a little higher? The woman positively reigned in that gown.

Rez exhaled. "That's the one."

"You like it?" The slide of her palm across the low neckline drew his eye.

Without shoes on, she was a good head and a half shorter than him. He took her hand and spun her before him. "Gorgeous."

She shrugged and then nodded, sheepishly accepting the compliment. "It makes me feel kind of pretty…"

"Kind of? You Americans! *Kind of… Sort of…*" He pulled her to him and kissed her. Soundly. "You are gorgeous. Full stop."

Her sigh dusted his neck. She ran a palm up his sleeve. He could feel her beginning another shrug, so he stopped her need to qualify and dismiss his desire to compliment her with another kiss.

This kiss accepted no excuses. It told her she was worthy and beautiful and that he was lucky to have her in his arms. The way her body melded against his when they kissed was a sensual treat. Her breasts were snug against his chest. Her closeness made him, oh, so hard. He wanted to devour her. To rip away the expensive lace and…

Viv parted herself from the kiss and whispered, "Good, then?"

"Très bien." There would be no lace-tearing. *Yet.* "Now, let's get you some shoes."

"Oh? Shoes…" She stepped away from his hold and rubbed a palm up her opposite arm. Her wince surprised him. "Yes, shoes."

Her mind had fled this dressing room. Rez could sense her taking a memory leap. Something with which he was all too familiar.

"What's going on in that beautifully lush brain of yours, Viv?"

She squeezed her eyelids shut. Was it that painful, then?

When finally she opened her eyes, she asked, "Did I tell you my husband used to call me Cinderella?"

"No." He was familiar with the fairy tale. "Was it to do with shoes?"

"Yes. You see, I have these weirdly narrow feet. I tend to step out of high heels. Often. So whenever it would happen my husband would shake his head and say, 'Did Cinderella lose her shoe again?' He'd retrieve the shoe and then bend down to put it back on me. Then he'd look up at me like Prince Charming and I'd lose my heart to him again. It's silly, but dressy shoes make me think of…well…. It was a special thing between the two of us."

"I understand," he said. And he did.

Couples shared personal things that no others would pick up on. It created an exclusivity that further bonded them. He and Colette had… Such frustration that their *thing* had slipped from his memory.

"But I don't think it would be appropriate to go barefoot."

Viv chuckled. "Of course I won't, you silly Frenchman." She looked over his shoulder to the salesclerk, who lingered out in the showroom. "Do you have anything that would go well with this dress? I'm a size seven. Not sure what that is in European sizes."

"Of course!" The clerk sailed off to retrieve some shoes.

Rez took Viv's hand and leaned in for another quick kiss. "This is almost fun."

"Shopping for women's clothes? It's fun for me. But it's not going to be fun for you once you get a glimpse of the price tag."

"Doesn't matter."

She rolled her eyes. "Your bank account must be incredible. I've never dated a millionaire before."

"Billionaire."

"Ah—really?"

She swallowed. And he knew the subject had to change.

"That doesn't matter, either. What does matter," he said, "is that this dress made you burst out of the dressing room like a beam of sunshine. It makes you happy."

"It does."

He kissed her forehead. "Mission accomplished."

* * *

The clerk returned with a pair of violet leather heels. Simple, but elegant.

"Shall I put them on for you?" the clerk asked.

"Uh…sure."

Viviane had slipped into a state of numbness. It struck her so quickly she merely reacted, lifting one foot and then the other as the woman gently slid the shoes onto her feet while Rez watched.

She couldn't determine if they were comfortable or they pinched because her mind was spinning. Not because she'd learned Rez was super-wealthy instead of merely wealthy. She could deal with that. *Maybe*. No, right now she was thinking about a fairytale princess and the handsome prince who had loved her for twenty-five years and then been stolen from her by a vile villain named cancer.

"Agréable?" the clerk asked. "I will leave you to walk in them and consider."

"Merci."

Still in a surreal haze of memory, Viviane walked toward the floor-length mirror and paused. The shoes hugged her feet snugly. They might always fit like that. Or they might become loosened the more she walked, and then…

She fled toward the dressing room, closing the door behind her, leaving Rez on the sofa, nursing his whiskey.

Meeting her gaze in the mirror, she saw the

first tear slip down her cheek. The voice from her past that she knew so well spoke to her.

"Did Cinderella step out of her shoe again? Sit, my love. There. It's perfect on you. I love you, Cinderella."

Viviane gasped out a few more tears, catching the back of her hand against her mouth. Brian had always treated her so tenderly, with genuine love. The shoe thing had been their shared moment. Even when shoes had fitted her well, she'd sometimes stepped out of one if she was in need of a hug. When she'd wanted to let Brian be the hero. The knight in shining armor who'd sweep in to save the princess.

She'd thought she'd gotten over all the dramatic emotional stuff following his death. The many days of crying. The times when memories would reduce her to tears while sitting at a stoplight. The sudden need to plunge her face against a sweater he'd worn, the one item of his clothing that she had saved. She'd never wash it. *Never.*

"Viviane?" Rez said softly from the other side of the door.

She lifted her head, swiping at a tear. "Just need a moment, please."

"Of course."

Rez was so kind. He understood her loss. He didn't push her and he never would. But what kind of crazy mess was she? Their first date had gone remarkably well. Now she intended to skip over the casual dating stage and go big by accompanying him to a *soirée*, of all things. A party where she had to be at her best. Fitting in with the wealthy and the famous.

That couldn't happen until she got her head on straight. Stopped running away when the smallest memory prodded her.

Looking down at the shoes, she decided they matched the gown perfectly. And they were comfortable. She could walk in them.

She shook her head. Who was she to attend a fancy ball at some fabulous Parisian landmark on the arm of a billionaire? That was so not in her wheelhouse.

But why not? she pleaded silently to her reflection.

She'd come to Paris to start something new. Why not an affair with a Frenchman? It was really happening. For the little time she might have in this city, why not play with the fantasy? She could do it. She had captured the Frenchman's attention. He wanted to take her to this party. The gown and shoes would make her look the part. Where was the strong, independent woman who was determined to grasp life?

I am here, she told herself, and lifted her head. Turning before the mirror, she studied herself front and sides. *I do look good. I love this color.* He had called her gorgeous. *Oh, Rez, I'm falling for you.*

She was not sure if that was good, bad, or stupid. Whatever it was, she was in for the ride.

Viv stepped out of the dressing room. Raising an arm while sliding the other hand down her hip, she embraced the sexy move. It felt...right.

"I can do this."

Rez pulled her into his arms. "Yes, you can."

The Le Beau boutique was still open when they arrived at around eight in the evening. The Champs-Élysées bustled with tourists, women walking tiny dogs, men sporting thick gold chains, crews of teenagers texting as they laughed, and families walking with heads turning and cell phones recording to take it all in. A bright yellow Lamborghini parked at the curb offered a chance for tourists to sit inside for a hefty price tag.

Rez quickly showed Viv around the shop. Massive crystal chandeliers hung over only a few jewelry display counters. Beautiful salespeople dressed in black smiled and greeted Rez warmly before he led Viv off the sales floor and down a narrow hallway. They went through a private doorway, then took the stairs up to the offices and workrooms.

Rez opened a bottle of wine and poured Viv a goblet. Not your standard office refreshments. Then he left her to wait in a private viewing room while he went to the walk-in safe to retrieve a few items.

Viviane imagined Le Beau's "big bucks" clients were probably led to this same room and served wine as they perused pricey baubles and bangles.

The furniture was antique Louis XV stuff, and the scent of designer perfume intoxicated her. The marble dais in the middle of the room must be for viewing the jewelry. A lighted mirror was the only thing on it.

She was excited to see what Rez would show her. He had insisted she borrow something to wear for the party, and how could she refuse?

A sip of wine confirmed that she might never again drink the cheap stuff. A girl could get used to wine that had been grown, fermented, and bottled only a hundred miles away. And the cheese here! And the walks in the beautiful parks! The entire city was walkable. Even if she lived here she might never see all there was to see.

Wouldn't that be a dream? To live in Paris? It was difficult to consider it, knowing her budget would never allow that. Yet she had knocked down the walls to her fantasy, so who was to know what other dreams might be accomplished? Fingers crossed, The Plant Whisperer business would take off and she'd be able to build a clientele in Europe. Because if not... It was home to Minnesota for this girl.

Rez returned with a black velvet tray and set it on the marble table. The glint of light on diamonds made Viviane gasp. One necklace lay on the tray. A pear-shaped diamond on a single strand. Classic and simple.

"Is that a pink diamond?" she asked.

"It is. It's elegant...not too heavy. It won't distract from your gown, and yet it will draw the eye."

Viv traced her finger over the cool, smooth diamond. The strand was made up of smaller diamonds, linked together. It was gorgeous.

"You designed this? You are so talented."

"*Merci*. That means a lot, coming from you."

"Now I understand why you don't want to walk away from this."

"This..." he tapped the necklace "...is my life. I can't imagine not designing jewelry. But this." He patted his thigh. The wounded leg. "Seems to freak Jean-Louis out."

"Your son wants you to leave Le Beau simply because of your limp? It's got to be more than that."

"I told you about the memory issues. Jean-Louis thinks I need to see a shrink."

"Oh. That's weird..."

On the other hand, she had read about people with traumatic brain injuries. It changed their lives—oftentimes dramatically. It could be difficult to deal with emotionally. Add to that the fact Rez had also lost his wife...

"And you don't want to do that?" she asked.

"Do I seem crazy to you?"

"You're not! But your son must have good reason to request such a thing of you."

"He wants to take over Le Beau. My brain injury is his excuse to do so."

"Hmm..."

She didn't want to intrude on a family battle. And with the necklace sparkling under her fingertips all she wanted was to fall into the dazzle and lose herself. On the other hand, Rez seemed mentally stable, even factoring in his grief. But she was no expert, and perhaps talking to someone about his medical condition would help.

"I'm sorry," Rez said. "It is for my son and I to discuss. Will you try this on?"

"I thought you'd never ask!"

He walked around behind her and she felt the weight of the heavy diamond land on her chest. Now, *that* was satisfying. Never had she worn diamonds—save her wedding ring set, which currently sat in a safe at home. Expensive jewels didn't appeal to her. Give her rhinestones any day.

And yet…

Viv leaned forward to inspect the necklace in the mirror. To say it dazzled like millions of stars was not exaggerating. *Wow.*

"You know," Rez said, leaning in near her shoulder, to meet her reflection in the mirror, "with this rock around your neck you won't need to stuff any in your bra for the party."

Viv laughed. "Oh, darling, I won't have a bra on that night."

He tilted his head. A brow lifted.

Whatever thoughts were going through his brain…she was all for it!

CHAPTER ELEVEN

CLAD IN THE LACY violet gown, Viv turned before the mirror, studying her backside. Still fit and trim. She had the body of a twenty-year-old. Very well, a twenty-year-old who'd been celebrating that birthday for thirty-some years, but still…

Not bad, she decided.

In fact, she felt great. The necklace Rez had loaned her had been delivered an hour earlier by a security car. Viv had been in the shower and found it on her bed when she'd come out. Opening the black velvet case had certainly been a Cinderella moment.

The pink diamond suited the dress—bigger than her thumb, it must be worth a bit. Best to be careful with it. Certainly if anything happened to it, it would come out of Rez's pocket. Though he was rich. Had billions…

She grabbed her cell phone and opened the internet browser. Then she set it down on the bed.

No, I won't snoop.

Financial status meant nothing to her. Seriously… A man could own all the fancy houses, cars, and suits in the world and still be a jerk. Rez was not a jerk.

But wow—did this diamond sparkle. She picked up the phone again.

Just a quick snoop.

Entering his name brought up a list of hits connected to Le Beau. Clicking on the image option filled the screen with Rezin Ricard's handsome mug. That man could work the tousled hair and stubble look. He always wore a suit, but had been captured in some easy poses that belied the staunch businessman and gave everyone a peek at the rebel she'd suspected lived within him. One of the photos featured him alongside a stunning woman with long dark hair and an incredible body clad in a dazzling silver gown. Her gravity-defying breasts could not be natural.

Must be his wife. Viv pressed her fingers to her lips. *Oh, my God, she is...was...a goddess. So beautiful. She must have been a model. Oh...*

Viv closed her eyes. What was she doing? Thinking she had any right to attend a fancy party, wearing an expensive gown and jewels, on the arm of a sexy billionaire who could date any woman he desired. Any young, beautiful, gorgeous woman.

She was no match for the cadre of women Rez must attract. Why was he taking *her* out tonight? It didn't make sense.

But appearance was not, and should not be, the most important thing in choosing a mate. Or a date. She and Rez had gotten to know one another and she was intrigued by the brain and the obvious creative talent behind the handsome face. And he had a sense of humor. And they'd kissed. A lot. She felt like they had become a couple. But he hadn't labeled her "girlfriend," and nor did she feel comfortable announcing to anyone that the man was her boyfriend.

And yet…

She sent another glance to the woman on his arm. Colette Ricard. She wasn't smiling. She wore one of those posed, pursed-lips looks that wouldn't cause a wrinkle. Most likely a model's conditioned reaction to the paparazzi. Rez wasn't holding her close or clasping her hand. It was as though she were the beauty on display and he wasn't allowed to muss her. What must that have been like? To do the public scene and put on a show for the cameras? Because Rez's smile wasn't all there, either. For some reason he looked distracted. Not happy.

Viv shook her head. She was imagining things. The couple had to have been married for as long as she and Brian had been if he had a son old enough to take control of the family business. Why hadn't she asked him?

Because he was still touchy about all things regarding his departed wife.

Had their relationship been loving and true? Or…something else?

"Viv?" Rez stood in the bedroom doorway. "I called your name. Are you okay?"

She tucked the phone behind her and stood. "Uh…maybe."

"You don't seem sure. Are you ready to leave—? *Wow*."

The sight of his open-mouthed expression flooded over her skin like a warm rain. His gaze devoured her. A lift of her chin had her basking in the adoration.

"You," he said in his husky baritone, "are stunning."

Viv didn't even fight the blush this time. It felt incredible to be admired. His look made her feel worthy of the expensive gown and jewels. Of him.

"I knew that diamond drop would go well with the gown," he said.

Certainly, though, she didn't measure up to Colette Ricard.

Viv rubbed her fingers up the back of her neck.

"What is it, Viv? There's something wrong. I know you."

"Do you really?"

Rez ran his palms down her arms. Goosebumps shivered in their wake.

Touch me more, she thought. *Everywhere. And make me believe this is real.*

For the first time she noticed his suit. A deep purple, almost black, the color barely noticeable had his bowtie not been edged with purple satin.

His hair wasn't so tousled and sexy as usual, now smoothed back and refined. She liked it no matter how he styled it.

Viv inhaled and closed her eyes. His usual leather tone was there, but it was topped with something sweeter—like cinnamon and maybe rum.

"Like something I could devour…"

"What?"

"Huh? Oh. Right. We were…uh…"

"Hey, I know I'm the one with the memory issues and dizziness, but are you sure you're all right to go out this evening?"

No, she wasn't. Pressing the flesh with celebrities and the moneyed elite was so out of her wheelhouse. She belonged with the plants, digging in the dirt, creating private escapes for other people.

On the other hand… Yes, she wanted to walk in on a handsome man's arm. To enjoy this beautiful gown and experience the life of the uber-rich and famous. Just for this one night. And then Cinderella would hitch a ride on a pumpkin—hopefully with both shoes still intact.

She wiggled her feet within the shoes. They fitted perfectly. But she hadn't walked in them much. Which had been her plan. She didn't want to stretch them and risk stepping out of one.

Viv inhaled courage and nodded. "I am more than all right. This dress makes me feel glamorous. The shoes are awesome. And my date is some kind of *GQ* model who smells absolutely edible."

He quirked a brow.

"It's your spicy cologne. I want to…" *Lick you.* "Well…"

Rez leaned in, nuzzling his nose along her jaw and into her hair. When his lips touched the top of her ear, Viv's entire skeletal structure went rubbery. Goosebumps again danced on her arms. And probably in her heart as well.

"I feel the same about you," he said in a husky whisper against her ear. "Whatever *'Well…'* entails, I'm all for it."

Another nuzzle, and he kissed her hair above her ear. Then her temple. Her eyebrow. He landed on her lips with the barest connection. A tease, really. For which she was thankful. She was not sure how her red lipstick would withstand anything too intense. She was not a big make-up wearer. Had never worried about kissing a man and then having to refresh her lipstick.

Oh, Viv, stop thinking and enjoy the man!

Threading her fingers through his soft, dark hair, she held him to her as they maintained a barely-there kiss. His scent seeped into her being. Their mingled breaths warmed skin and lips. Her lashes dusted his face.

He smiled against her mouth, and then broke the ethereal moment. "That lipstick…" he murmured.

"Too much?"

Oh, no. She'd thought it might be too bright, inappropriate. She would stick out like a—

"Exquisite," Rez whispered against her mouth. "It lures me. You are making promises to me, Viv, do you know that?"

"I…uh…" *Why the heck not? Relax!* "I'm not big on breaking promises."

He pulled back, his smile soft and sensual. "I'll remember that. But only make those promises to me, *oui*?"

"Deal. So," she said, "is this another date? I mean, what are you going to say when you introduce me to people tonight?"

"This is a date." He shrugged. "That you're my girlfriend?"

She twined her fingers in his. "You don't sound very sure of that."

"I'm *not* sure. This is…"

"I know." She closed her other hand over their clasped hands and looked up to his bowed gaze. "This is new for both of us." He nodded. "Let's let it go where it wants and wing it."

"That works for me. But…uh… Jean-Louis will be there. I may have to introduce you as…"

"You can call me a friend, if you think he'll be upset to see his father with a woman."

"He may…he may not be. He's aware I've tried a few dates and he didn't say anything about them. Probably because he knew they were failures. For all I know he wants his old man to get a girlfriend to keep him occupied and make him want to leave the company."

Viv clasped his hand firmly. "No arguments with your son tonight, okay? You need to be the calm, cool patriarch of Le Beau. Don't give Jean-Louis any fodder for this silly business of labeling you incapable."

"That sounds like a plan. We'll see how good I am at carrying it out. Lately when Jean-Louis and I speak it always ends in an argument."

"Then perhaps you should carry a glass of champagne with you all night."

Rez regarded her curiously.

"If you feel the need for heated words coming on—sip."

"Sip?" He chuckled. "Or maybe I should keep you to hand? I'd rather kiss your gorgeous mouth than sip champagne."

"I like the sound of that."

His next kiss was too quick. "Now, what was going on with you when I came in here? You were distracted."

Viv sighed and grabbed her phone. She showed him the screen, which was still open to the images page. "I'm sorry. I was curious about you and Le Beau so I did a search. Then I saw a photo of you with your wife. She was so beautiful."

"She was. But how did that upset you? You're the one who has been teaching me about leaning into grief and accepting it for what it is."

"It's not that. She's… I just got down on myself. Didn't think I could hold a candle to an obviously stunning model. I know I don't measure up—"

This time Rez's kiss was firm and not at all gentle. His mouth commanded hers. His fingers in her hair gripped, holding her to him. *Silence*, the kiss said. *It's only the two of us. Don't allow a ghost to be your rival.* And when Viv was finally able to think again she'd forgotten what the topic had been.

"Good," Rez said as he took her hand. "You needed that diversion. Now, I have a date with a gorgeous woman who makes silent promises with every curl of her lips. And we are going to have fun tonight. *Oui?*"

She nodded. *"Oui."*

The driver stopped before the Grand Palais, which was not far from the mansion, but if Viv had had to walk that distance in those shoes… Well, forget it!

Rez, *sans* cane, got out and offered his hand to help her out. Paparazzi milled. Camera flashes dazzled. And all the French shouts were likely commands to *Look this way!* or *Pose!* as arriving couples complied.

And—wow!—a real red carpet stretched up the stairs toward the entrance doors.

A man approached Rez and shook his hand.

They seemed to know one another. The man was tall and brutish, like a brawler, and Viv could see a neck tattoo peeking out from his shirt.

Rez leaned in to say, "This is Victor. He's your security for the evening."

"My—?" Suddenly unsure, Viv touched the necklace. The cool diamond wobbled over her skin. "Seriously? Because of the necklace?"

"It's standard. He won't bother you, but he will shadow you." His cheek brushing hers, and his back to the crowd of photographers, Rez asked, "Still okay about all this?"

"Maybe…"

"You're fiddling with that diamond like you're not okay."

She stopped. "Sorry. It must be worth tens of thousands. I'll be careful with it."

"Thousands?" Rez whistled low. "That pink diamond is worth one point five million."

Viv grasped his hand at the same time as her brain processed that information. In her peripheral vision a camera flash blinded her. And suddenly they were walking toward a clutter of clicking cameras and shouting paparazzi.

With a glance over her shoulder she saw Victor follow, hands folded before him, eyes scanning. But all she could think was—*What the heck?* She was wearing over a million dollars' worth of diamond around her neck. It was more than she'd ever see in her back account. How could Rez trust her with such an item? What if it got lost? Fell off her?

Rez paused at the doors to the palace and nodded to everyone. He waved and squeezed her hand. Viv managed a smile. Not sure how she did it. She was moving on automatic pilot, not processing anything but the blur of camera flashes.

Do not pass out.

As they walked inside the main foyer, leaving behind the rush of photographers, Viv exhaled, and this time when Rez squeezed her hand she squeezed back.

"I wish you'd told me how much this necklace is worth before you loaned it to me," she said on a chiding whisper.

They were approaching a lavish reception area decorated with white gardenias and trailing pale green strings of pearl succulents.

"Would you have worn it if I had?"

"Never!"

"Exactly. Viv, are you having some kind of—how do you say it?—a freak-out?"

"Possibly."

"Do you need me to slap you?"

"What? Are you serious? No." She laughed. "Sorry. You're right." Dropping the diamond and smoothing both palms over her hips, she straightened and lifted her chin. "Victor will always be close?"

"That's what I pay him for."

"Fine. I can do this."

"Of course you can. I never doubted you for a moment. What do you say we do this together?"

And the night began.

CHAPTER TWELVE

THE GRAND PALAIS had been built as an exhibition hall for the 1900 Universal Exposition. It combined the Baroque with Classicism in its steel framework, copious windows and glass dome. Chanel frequently held its runway shows there, under the dome. The Ricards would not have considered any other venue for this celebration.

Viv whispered to Rez as she took it all in, "It's amazing. Massive. And yet the place manages to feel intimate and warm, like a greenhouse."

"Then you should feel right at home this evening. Let's do the circuit, shall we?"

Rez kept Viv on his arm as he wandered through the glass-domed nave, greeting every face and thanking people as he recalled a piece he had made for them or the many pieces designed by Le Beau over the years and enjoyed by their families. He introduced Viv simply as Viviane Westberg.

It felt odd to have a woman at his side who was not Colette. And as he approached friends, they initially gave Rez a startled look, which then quickly segued into a smile. They all knew he'd lost his wife. Did they think it was too soon for him to have someone new in his life? Were they happy for him?

It shouldn't bother him, but anxiety was keeping him from completely relaxing. Time for more champagne.

Viv's fingers fluttered to the pink diamond often. He wished she would just own it—just for the evening. The truly dazzling thing was the woman wearing the diamond. And she was a real trooper as she stood at his side, listening to the mostly French conversation. Though he did start all his introductions in English, people naturally flowed into their native language.

It took a while to work the room, and as he collected another goblet of champagne for the two of them Viv veered him toward the displays in the center of the room. A whole room had been constructed of large drawings of his designs. Its walls reminded him of the Japanese *shoji* screens.

Viv broke from his arm to study the drawings. Rez stood proudly behind her, stunned that she'd even have an interest in them. Not once had she indicated this *soirée* was boring, but for him…? A hundred years was an awesome accomplishment. But, much as he enjoyed seeing clients, having to be "on" and schmooze was not his thing.

It had once been his thing. Or had it been Colette's milieu and he'd been at ease only by her side? Now that he considered it, he had to concede that truth. His wife had been his social crutch. Which made him realize that he could relate to Viviane's nervousness even more.

A glance to his right noted his son, dressed in a tuxedo and chatting animatedly with one of Le Beau's most faithful clients. Rez felt his anxiety rise—but then he breathed out. Because as he watched Jean-Louis he was overcome with a certain pride. Pride that his son was standing there, displaying to the world the professionalism and elegance that were the cornerstones of Le Beau. As Jean-Louis shook hands with the client, he laughed heartily. And a small turn found him acknowledging another client, whom Rez knew had flown in from Berlin specifically for this event.

Perhaps Rez had not considered how comfortable Jean-Louis was with all aspects of the company. *Mon Dieu*, he needed to sort out his life—and his issues with Jean-Louis. He had to get back to his normal self, which included being social and enjoying life. There had simply been too much upheaval lately. Le Beau and his jewelry design was the one thing that had remained consistent. He couldn't walk away from that anchor.

Viv was slowly walking along the wall of drawings. "You drew all of these?"

"Yes. Apparently Penelope let Jean-Louis into my drawings cabinet. They do look good blown up to poster-size. She's going to hang some in the shop also."

Viv turned a beaming smile at him. "They look as good as the real thing. You can catch the sparkle of the diamonds and the blood-red glint in the ruby. And I love the aquamarine. Where do you get your inspiration?"

Her compliments straightened his shoulders more than he'd thought possible. Some of his anxiety slipped away. "Everywhere. I love symmetry, nature, beauty. Sometimes the stones seem to design themselves."

"I can understand that. Same with plants. Sometimes I just follow where they want me to go."

"You are an artist as well."

"I suppose a little."

Americans and their need to downplay their accomplishments! Hadn't she mentioned something about once winning an award for her work?

"It must be satisfying to see your work worn by nearly every woman in attendance tonight," she said.

"Absolutely. I love it."

He kissed her hand. She smelled like the garden. How she managed that, he wasn't sure, but it was wild and fresh, and he wanted to kiss her deeply—right now.

"Look at that one!" She approached a drawing of an elaborate blue sapphire and diamond choker he'd designed for Colette's fortieth birthday.

Rez lifted his chin, fighting his need to turn away, to ignore anything that tugged at his memory. Yet the night of the accident was still a black hole. So he should appreciate any memory that came to him, shouldn't he?

He walked up behind Viviane and slid his hands over her hips. "I made that for Colette." Saying her name was growing easier. "She loved sapphires. The center stone is forty carats. The diamonds laddering along the stone are black. She screamed when she opened the box on the morning of her fortieth birthday."

Viv's tilted her head back onto his shoulder and Rez realized she belonged there, close to him. She didn't intrude on his memories; she helped him to own them, to embrace them. To simply allow them to exist.

"How much is it worth?" she asked.

"Eighteen million."

"Oh, dear… I can't imagine the security detail that must have surrounded *her.*"

Rez wrinkled a brow. Why did the mention of Colette and her security guard make him feel anxious suddenly? He hadn't seen the man who had so often flanked Colette when they attended events in years. He'd left Rez's employment while he'd been recuperating in the hospital.

Viv turned and looked up at him. "Sorry. Here we go…talking about our spouses again."

"It's okay." He shook off the unnerving sensation of lost memory. "But I would suggest that this *is* a party. And I do see the champagne server heading our way."

They switched their empty goblets for full ones again, and as Rez sipped he noticed someone wave across the room.

"That's a Scandinavian prince. I'm designing his fiancée's wedding set. I should speak to him."

"Of course! This is your party. I don't want to monopolize you. Leave me to finish looking at all your drawings. I'll be fine. But please know I won't be able to keep my eyes off you."

"I love being your focus," Rez said.

She leaned in and whispered at his ear. "When I look at you, I lose all interest in what's going on around me."

He shivered as she slowly brushed her lips across his cheek. Not a kiss. Something so much more. She'd marked him. And her hush of breath burned deep into his being.

Viv placed her full champagne goblet on a passing server's tray. She had already consumed one glass, and the giddy feeling dancing in her brain was not entirely because she was living out a fantasy tonight. Time to cut herself off. Before she did something embarrassing. She had only been drunk a couple times in her life. It had never ended well.

Stopping before the final drawing, which featured a star design in the center of a tiara, she glanced around. Victor wasn't far behind. Not at all creepy in his constant surveillance, remarkably he blended into the background noise. Good guy.

Man, this place was amazing. It was all so open and airy. And it really did feel like a greenhouse. Though the sky had darkened above, the lighting dazzled like stars along the overhead steel framework.

"Lovely, yes?"

Viv turned at the sound of an obvious American accent and smiled at a young couple. The woman sported a head of dark, thick braids coiled in a beehive, while her husband's dreadlocks were corralled behind his head in a ponytail.

"These drawings are amazing," Viv said. "You two are…visiting Paris?"

"We just purchased a home in the Sixteenth," the woman excitedly announced. She offered her hand to Viv to shake. "I'm Evangeline, and this is my husband, Nestor. Nestor is a cutter for Le Beau. Just hired last year."

Viv touched the pink diamond at her throat. "You are so lucky to work with Le Beau. Their designs are beautiful."

"Nestor loves beauty," Evangeline said. "Now we want to bring that beauty into our new home. We're too excited about it all."

Viv smiled, but she noticed Nestor appeared… bored.

"The painting and the new furniture," Evangeline went on enthusiastically. "And we must find a gardener!"

"A gardener?" Viv's heart double-thumped. "I'm a gardener. I have over twenty years' experience. Do you have an established garden or are you looking to create one?"

"It's established on the terrace, but it needs much work. My goodness, we must exchange contact info. We don't move in for weeks, but I would love to learn more about what you do."

Viv gave the woman her number, and when Nestor nudged his wife toward the refreshments bar she waved the twosome off. A possible client?

"Good job, Viviane," she whispered to herself.

A sweeping glance about the room saw that Rez had moved on to another couple. He stood out in the crowd—tall, dark, the proverbial handsome prince. In fact he carried himself as if he were a king. Truly, he was the patriarch of Le Beau. She hoped his son would not succeed in forcing him away from something he loved so much. This was his element, standing amidst the beauty and elegance that he had created.

She couldn't wait to get him home and kiss him silly. He was her man. If only for the night.

At the sight of something troubling, Viv clenched her fingers. Rez's arm had reached out, his fingers grasping. The people he was speaking to didn't notice. But she knew exactly what that subtle movement meant. He was feeling unsteady.

Weaving her way through the partygoers, she smiled at all the women and men she passed. Whatever they muttered in French about the oddball woman on the rich jeweler's arm didn't matter. There was only one opinion in this room that she cared about. And he preferred to call her strange.

As she reached Rez's side she smiled at the couple he was speaking to. Unobtrusively, she slid a hand up Rez's back. His spine melded firmly against her palm. She sensed his weight shift from foot to foot, and then to both as he found a steady stance.

"I should introduce you to my date," Rez said in English to the couple. "This is Viviane Westberg. Viviane, this is Maxine and Thierry Robalt."

Maxine bussed Viv's cheeks, then displayed the huge red rock on her middle finger. "Rezin designed this little bauble for me. Burmese ruby. Adorable, isn't it?"

"Oui." Adorable? It was as large as a gumball that surely would cause a child to choke. "Rez's designs are *incroyable*." Viv tried a bit of French.

"Très incroyable!"

They exchanged some pleasantries about the event and the displays, and then the couple wandered off. She and Rez were immediately approached by a man who observed Viviane with the cautious eye of a vulture sitting on a bare branch above a dying soul. The man had unruly dark curly hair that seemed to want to take control of his head. Blue eyes startled her with recognition. And when they dropped to take in the pink diamond his jaw tightened.

"Jean-Louis," Rez said in introduction. "This is Viviane Westberg. She's been refurbishing the garden at Colette's *tanière*."

Viv squeezed Rez's hand at the mention of his wife. She knew it took a lot for him to utter the name.

"My mother loved that garden," Jean-Louis said. His discerning gaze flickered over Viv's face, her shoulders—then back to the pink diamond. "You must do it justice."

"I will. And I am," she added.

"She is," Rez reassured. "She's not changed the layout or your mother's roses."

"The roses… *Oui*."

Jean-Louis noticeably swallowed. He lifted his chin in a Rez-like move that Viv knew indicated a staunch need not to show emotion.

"Interesting… You two are friends? To be here… together?"

Viv knew exactly what the man was angling at. Was she dating his father? Were they sleeping together? It wasn't her place to say anything, when it was Rez who must carefully guard his interactions against a son who wanted to wrest away the family company from him should he make one misstep. And that misstep had been prevented by her hand to his back.

"We are together this evening," Rez offered.

"And she's wearing the pink," Jean-Louis stated accusingly.

"She does it justice, *oui*?"

Then Rez said something in French to Jean-Louis. It didn't sound chastising or accusatory, just matter-of-fact. *Mind your own business*? Viv could hope for that...

"I wanted to share this amazing event with Viv, who is doing something wonderful for our family."

"Of course, Papa."

But Viv could see Jean-Louis wasn't buying it. Her heart dropped a notch. Rez hadn't claimed her as a girlfriend or even his date. She was a friend whom he wanted to thank for doing a job. *Ugh*. Had she expected more? Yes. But she could allow Rez that omission to his son. She'd stepped into the middle of a family battle. Best to stand as far out of the line of fire as possible.

"Are you going to stay for the DJ?" Jean-Louis asked his dad.

"The what?"

"Music, Papa. We're going to drop the lights at midnight and bring up the music. The stuffy part of the evening will come to a close."

Viv noticed Rez's jaw tighten.

"I love a rousing dance floor," she tried.

"You're not going to play that ridiculous club music?" Rez asked.

"It may be ridiculous to you, but our younger and richer clients love it. You must stay. Get a good feel for the clientele Le Beau must romance in order to remain relevant."

It seemed a heavy exhalation was all Rez could manage. Viv wanted to hold him. Reassure him. But instead she slid her hand up his back again—this time not to support him, but merely to convey *I understand.*

"Whatever you decide…" Jean-Louis turned and nodded to someone across the room. "Remember, you left the planning of this party in *my* hands. And the guests are loving it. Now, I've to make sure the set-up is ready to go. Good evening, Papa." He nodded at Viv, but said nothing to her in parting as he wandered into the crowd.

Rez turned to follow his son's leaving. Viv pressed both palms to his back. His tension was palpable even through the suit coat.

"Want to stay and dance?" she suggested.

When he turned toward her she wasn't sure if he was looking at her or fuming. At the very least she was thankful he had not started a vocal argument with Jean-Louis.

"Or we could leave now." She glanced to the big clock hanging above the balcony. "Almost midnight."

He grinned. "You know, I used to stay out until morning, dancing and drinking."

"Oh, yeah? I've never drunk much, but I can dance. I'm feeling the champagne, for sure."

"I feel as if I stay for the music it'll only drive my anxiety further into the red zone."

She clasped his hand. "I can sense that."

"You won't be upset if we leave now?"

"Why should I be? I've had the best evening. But can the CEO of Le Beau leave his own party early?"

"The CEO can do whatever he damn well pleases." He held out his arm and she took it with hers. "I've had enough schmoozing and pressing the flesh. Now I want to focus on the best part of this night. You."

Lifted by that compliment, Viv followed Rez and they made their way out of the building. It took a while. Rez politely paused to thank people and converse briefly with them when they recognized him walking by. But once they stood outside, at the top of the stairs, Viv inhaled the sweet night air, perfumed with the white gardenias.

In the background the beat of a rap song pounded through the open doorway.

"We'll dance back at the mansion," Rez said. "You like slow dancing?"

"Sounds like my speed."

As they stepped down the staircase, arm in arm, Rez pulled out his cell phone. "I'll call Henri.

He's always close. We'll stop by Le Beau on the way to the mansion. I imagine you won't mind me locking up that necklace for the evening?"

"I've grown fond of it, actually. But I'm sure Victor would like to be relieved of his duties as well, so he can return to the party and dance."

Rez smirked and wandered down a few steps.

Viv suddenly let out a cry of dismay. Stopping abruptly, she lifted the purple lace skirt.

Seriously? After she'd been so careful all evening?

Stopping and holding his phone against his chest, Rez bent to study her face. "What's wrong, *mon amour*?"

She forced a smile. "You'll never believe this…"

"What? Do you want to go back inside? If you don't want to miss the dancing—"

"It's not that at all. It's just…" She turned and gestured to the violet leather shoe on the step behind her. "I've stepped out of my shoe."

"Oh." He met her gaze in the glow of the festive party lights. Then his expression smoothed, and he said more seriously, "Oh…"

Viviane's shoulders dropped. *Really? This was happening now?* She had been having a great time—hadn't given one moment of thought to her husband—and now…

"Got it." Rez patted her shoulder and directed her to sit down on the wide step covered with red carpeting. "You sit here." When she was comfortable, he retrieved the shoe and handed it to her. "This is yours. And I…" he again took out his cell phone "…am going to call Henri."

He bent to meet her gaze at eye level. For a moment she could feel his concern like a palpable squeeze to her heart. No kiss was necessary. She could read reassurance in his intense blue eyes.

"I'll leave you to it. You going to be okay?"

Shoe in hand, Viv nodded, fighting the burgeoning tears. "I am."

He stepped away, taking the last few stairs and disappearing around the corner to where the limos were parked. Victor held his post at the bottom of the staircase.

Viv clutched the violet shoe to her chest. The misplaced midnight shoe. Cinderella's folly. Suddenly, in a moment when she'd thought to be horrified by the replay of something that had been so special to her and Brian, she could only smile against the leather shoe. Rez had not offered to put on the shoe for her. Because he knew what that meant to her. He'd honored the memory of her husband so exquisitely.

As a tear spilled down her cheek, reality pierced her heart. She loved Rez for his discretion and kindness. The Prince had won this damsel's respect and trust. Now could he win her heart?

CHAPTER THIRTEEN

THE DROP-OFF AT Le Beau did not take long. Victor escorted Rez inside with the diamond necklace while Viviane waited in the car with Henri. Indeed, the security guard did intend to head back to the party for "the sick tunes," as he'd stated during the ride.

Henri drove them back to the mansion through a surprising amount of traffic that made the trip a slow go.

Rez was not so much tired as disappointed. And not even with Jean-Louis. He did understand what his son was trying to do because he wanted to move Le Beau in a new direction. What baffled Rez was that *he* felt so resistant to it. It wasn't as though he couldn't maintain the elegance and status of the company while Jean-Louis injected some new blood and new marketing. They could possibly create a new division, focused toward the bling and the hip designs that appealed to the younger set.

Was he fighting it for another reason? Sure, he hated being considered an invalid by his son. He had been laid up in bed for weeks following the accident, then had used a walker for another few weeks, and a cane for almost a year following. Now he had his good days and bad days. But mentally he was all there.

The thing was, how would he know he'd forgotten something if he didn't get any reminders of that forgotten thing? And what of the things about his life that he couldn't remember?

Well, he sensed he and Colette had been heading in a bad direction the few years before the accident. He had loved her. Without question. But what about her? It drove him mad to think about it.

Viviane's asking about Colette's security guard had nudged at him. Boris, who had been Colette's personal guard, had left Paris after the accident. Rez had not heard from him except to be told he'd collected his final paycheck from Penelope.

But his marriage issues had nothing to do with controlling Le Beau. Had his reluctance to kowtow to Jean-Louis's suggestions got something to do with the fact that if he turned over control of the company then he'd be left with nothing? He'd lost his wife. What had he got left? He could not lose his grasp on the one last thing that meant something to him.

"We're here."

Viv's voice jarred him from his defeatist thoughts. He did now have an amazing woman in his life. That was something. That was a lot. But she wouldn't be in Paris for much longer. Did he have any right to ask her to stay? Was he ready for a commitment like that?

"You okay?" Viv asked.

Rez lifted his head. Rain spattered the window. He knew Henri, who had an umbrella, would bring it around and meet them at the passenger door.

"You seemed lost there," she said. "Didn't hear Henri the first time he asked if you wanted the umbrella."

Really? Maybe he *was* losing his grasp. "My mind was wandering. Sorry. I'm back now." He kissed the back of Viv's hand. "A lot of stuff going on tonight, eh?"

"Très bien."

He chuckled. "That means *very good* not *a lot*."

"Oh, well, then…yes, a lot."

The door opened. Rez took the umbrella and walked Viv slowly toward the entrance gate, knowing those shoes of hers might fall off at any time. Narrow feet? Apparently so.

When he'd looked back to see her shoe on the step, and then at her face—Cinderella, heartbroken—he'd known he couldn't help her. It wasn't his place. And he didn't want it to be his place. He didn't want to spoil her husband's memory.

But he did want to be in her life. He knew that now, more than ever, especially after what she'd done for him tonight.

He entered the digital code and once inside the mansion set down the umbrella and shook off the rain from his sleeves. Viv wandered ahead, stepping out of her shoes halfway to the stairs, where she turned and spread out her arms.

"Tonight was a fantasy come to life," she announced with a spin.

Of course wearing a beautiful gown and a pink diamond would be appealing for any woman. But for him...? The fantasy of being understood and accepted was all he needed.

He crossed the room and kissed her red lips. Her body melted against his. He had forgotten what it felt like to hold a woman. To taste her mouth and receive what she wanted to give him. It had been too long. Much longer than the two years since his wife had passed. Because, yes, he and Colette had been experiencing distance—and, no, he wouldn't let those thoughts rise. Now was for enjoying Viviane.

He spun her around and Viv tugged him to a stop. "There's a light on in the conservatory. Would you mind getting me some water while I run to turn it off?"

"Sure. No champagne?"

"I've reached my limit. I'm feeling a little..."

"Drunk?"

"Relaxed... And a little disoriented. I just need to regroup."

"I'll meet you in the garden."

* * *

The chandelier cast a soft glow over the back circle of the conservatory. Viviane wandered inside, her bare feet taking the cool tiles lightly. The Paris sky was dark, but beneath the chandelier the newly pruned greenery gleamed.

She paused and closed her eyes. What a dream this night had been. And while Cinderella had peeked out for a look, the woman who had been rescued on those stairs was not that princess anymore. She was a woman who had taken a chance on a new life and who was currently flying. Everything felt perfect. So much so that she wanted to…

Slipping her cell phone from her purse, she opened the music app. Her favorite playlist? *Click.*

Tilting back her head, she swept out her arms and swayed to the music. A turn allowed her to spy Rez standing in the garden's entrance. He'd loosened his tie and his hair was now tousled the way she preferred it. Her rescuing knight in Armani armor.

She crooked her finger. "You said you wanted to dance with me?"

Setting the water bottle on the floor, he walked over and slid his hands down her hips. He studied her gaze as languorously as his hands studied her body, moving slowly over her hips and up her waist…just under her breasts. Her nipples tightened. She gasped and her entire body arched toward him. Then he took her hands in his.

A new song began, with a lone guitar plucking a bass beat. The slow tune was sung by a woman with a country twang.

"I love this one." She hugged up against Rez's body, head tilted against his shoulder. "It's called 'Girl Crush.'"

"Crushing a girl?" he asked in a wondrous soft baritone.

She laughed. "To have a crush on someone is to desire them...to moon over them."

"Ah, yes, then I have a crush, too. She is a beautiful nymph who lives in a conservatory and likes to seduce me with her cooking."

Viv's entire body took in that compliment with a frisson and a sigh. Clasping her hands against his chest, Rez bowed his head over hers. They swayed in a slow circle beneath the spectacle of crystals and foliage. This was her fantasy, away from the crowds, listening to a man's heartbeat, melding against his heat. She needed him. She wanted him. Every part of her being pleaded for him.

When the song got to the part about tasting her lips, Rez tilted up her chin and kissed her. Softly. And deeply. This was right. *They* were right.

He bowed his forehead to hers. "Thank you for what you did for me tonight, Viv."

"I didn't do anything for you."

"*Oui*, you did. I felt your hand at my back when I needed it most. I needed support and you were there for me."

Another kiss. He tasted like champagne and new beginnings.

"I want to make love with you, Viv."

Her mouth opened in surprise, yet her heart twinkled. "Me too."

He held out his hand. "Let's go to my room. I want you to see the view on this rainy midnight."

He hadn't been kidding about the view. The second-floor bedroom was massive, and one wall was all windows. Viv stood before the window, peering across the river at the Eiffel Tower. Strung with twenty thousand lights, the Iron Lady twinkled as much as Viv's heart did.

Life felt wondrous.

When Rez embraced her from behind, she tilted back her head, inhaling leather and desire. His hand slid up from her waist to cup her breast. Mmm… She loved that he handled her as if he had every right to do so. Because he did.

He kissed along her neck, up to her earlobe. Marking her, exploring her with his warm breath and gentle kisses.

"I'm only going to ask once," he said, "and then we're not going to bring it up for the rest of the night."

"Sounds serious…but go for it."

He stepped around in front of her, kissed her hand and held it to his chest. "Are you okay with this?"

She knew what he was asking. Was she okay with *this*? *This* having sex with a man who was not her husband. Getting intimate on a whole new level. Stepping out of her shoes and into a new adventure.

Well, she'd already stepped out of her shoes…

"I am more than okay. What about you?"

He threaded his fingers through her hair. "Very okay with it."

CHAPTER FOURTEEN

THE FIRST THING Viviane saw when she opened her eyes to the morning light was the Eiffel Tower surrounded by a robin's-egg-blue sky. Add to that view the fact that she lay on sheets that must have cost a mint. That the pillow under her head was softer than a goose's butt, but still supportive. And the sheets smelled like spice and sex… Life could not get any better.

No handsome Frenchman beside her, though. She suspected Rez had wandered to the bathroom, which was a long stroll across the marble floor. The apartment she'd left back home, plopped above a shoe shop, would easily fit into this bedroom.

What a crazy dream. And she was living it! Frenchman included.

Rolling onto her side and tugging up the sheet, she closed her eyes, sinking into bliss. She had had sex. After years of self-imposed but not necessarily wanted chastity. And it had been perfect.

What made her smile, though, was that she didn't feel guilty about it. She deserved this. But she wondered if Rez felt the same way. Did he feel guilty about having sex with a new woman? She hoped not.

The man was a pretty easy read. He still carried a lot of attachment to his wife. If this had been a one-night thing for him, then she could deal with it. Maybe. She really liked Rez. Heck, the man who had handed her her shoe last night had realized this damsel had specific memories that must not be trampled by a new knight. It had been a long time since she felt so respected, so...*seen*.

She could fall in love with Rez. Maybe she already had.

Could this affair become a real relationship? A *Why don't you spend more than a night with me and move in?* kind of thing?

It felt like an option to Viv. Of course she was high on the vibes of new sex and passion. But she was not beyond going there. Life had decided to lead her into Rez's bed last night, and she intended to continue to follow that lead.

How? That was the question. She didn't even live on the same continent as the man. And there was the dead wife. Could she compete with a ghost? Rez still showed signs of reluctance to move on from his grief. Not that she expected him never to think of his lost spouse again.

The bed was jostled beside her. Rez's hand swept along her waist and down her thigh. Strong fingers squeezed her leg and he pressed his groin against her buttocks. He nuzzled in near her shoulder. But then she felt him pull back for a few seconds.

"What's wrong?" Viv asked.

"Twelve," he said.

"Twelve?"

"Freckles on your shoulders. And so many more down...here..." He nipped her waist, and then her buttock, and then hugged her. "So, what were you thinking about that I was able to sneak up on you?"

"Where I belong," she answered without pause. She wanted to be honest with him. And they did need to know where they stood in this liaison. "Paris is not my home."

He rolled onto his back and Viv turned over to face him. His body was lean, but taut with muscle. The scar on his leg ran from hip to thigh. He'd flinched when she'd touched it last night, and she knew it was more from embarrassment than pain. No need to bother him about that. There were many other, more interesting parts of him...

Oh, baby, did he have a nice penis. Nothing about him screamed *I'm old and can't get it up.* Nor did it indicate he was aging out of his job and couldn't mentally handle the CEO position anymore.

On the other hand, if he was *not* CEO he could travel. With her.

"What happened last night?" she asked.

He turned toward her. Such inquisitive blue eyes. They matched the sky this morning.

"I mean, with us," she added. "This. The sex."

"The sex was awesome."

"It was. But was it a one-night thing or...? Well?"

He exhaled through his nose and trailed a finger along her hairline. "What do you want it to be, *mon amour*?"

"I'm not sure. You tell me what you want out of this."

"Viv, I thought we were playing it day by day?"

"We are." Dared she tell him she was considering them committing to one another? Becoming a real couple? Could she have a relationship and still create her dream job?

"Then let's keep doing that," he said.

Men. So afraid of commitment—or even simple plans! "But what about when I leave? The garden is close to completion."

"I can pay overtime."

"Are you saying you'd *pay* me to stay longer? Not sure I like the sound of that."

"I didn't mean it that way. I like what happened last night. I'd like it to happen again."

She kissed his shoulder. "Me too."

"So can we continue to play it by ear?"

It wasn't the answer she wanted. But what *did* she want to hear?

Oh, please, Viv, I adore you and I want you to stay with me forever?

Or even: *No, one night was enough. Let's go back to employer and employee.*

Either one didn't feel realistic right now. But she did like to have a plan. A destination.

The old Viviane liked plans. You're trying something new, remember?

Viv stretched an arm across Rez's chest and hugged him. "Okay. We'll do the day-by-day thing. And today is Sunday—which is my day off."

"Want to take a walk and pick up some croissants? Or…?"

"Or?"

"We could make love again."

"That's a tough decision."

"Really?" He genuinely looked hurt.

"Why don't we do both?"

"I do love a woman who knows what she wants."

Her heart knew what she wanted. But her logical side hadn't caught up just yet.

A private park a block from the mansion hugged the Seine. Rez set his cane to one side of the wooden bench. He and Viv had purchased *crêpes* from a vendor. The sweet treats oozed with bananas and chocolate hazelnut spread. He hadn't had one of these since his teen years. He'd forgotten how indulgent they were. And messy.

Viv finished hers in record time, then sprang up to look over the river.

The day was perfect. Their relationship felt fresh,

vital, and open to so much opportunity. It was like beginning a new design on paper. The drawing stage was the most exciting because anything could happen.

He'd done it! He'd dove in this time and hadn't fled when the date had got to the part where he'd had to kiss the woman. He'd taken her home and they'd had crazy good sex. No doubt about it— he and Viv were a sexual match.

And thinking about it… He hadn't forgotten anything about Viv. Not even the smallest detail—like the name of that weird destructive plant, or her scent, or even that she held conversations with cats. Interesting… It was as if his brain had decided she was important to remember.

But she wasn't in Paris forever. And while he'd dodged her question about what they were doing earlier, he did have to face the fact she wouldn't be around for much longer. Dare he risk his heart for a short-lived fling? What if he wanted her to stay longer? He could set her up in an apartment close to his place… If her business goal succeeded—and he suspected it would; she was smart—she could travel and then return home to him.

He couldn't tell her about that idea. She'd be offended. Convinced he wanted to pay for her to stay in his life. If he was honest with himself, it sounded suspiciously like he wanted to keep her as a mistress. And that was not what he wanted, either. Yet he did want her near. Always.

Viv's non-judgmental presence gave him renewed confidence. Her hand at his back had been the most affirming thing he'd gotten from a woman. Ever. He and Viv related on terms that were new to him. Not so superficial as he and Colette, but deep. They could simply be near one another without talking and be comfortable. Like now.

Yet would she be content with a man who intended to remain where he was? In Paris. Working every day at his passion. Her job description seemed to require that she live a nomadic life. That part of her didn't fit with him. Certainly, he did enjoy traveling. But…hmm… Did Viv's adventurous dream mean this could only be a fling?

No, what they had begun was surely something more. Was he willing to relinquish some of his control at Le Beau in order to gain time with her? That was what must happen if he wanted this relationship to work. And he wanted to make the effort to show her he was ready to…well, to *love* her.

Viv returned to the bench, excitedly telling him about the anchored barges that lined the shore. She tilted her head onto his shoulder. *Bateaux Mouches* filled with tourists floated by on the silvery river's waves. Butterflies stitched the air. And somewhere a duck quacked.

Rez had not felt so free and relaxed in a long time. And he liked this feeling.

Monday morning felt full of possibilities. Until. Sitting behind his desk, Rez noticed the pink slip of paper that must have been placed there by Penelope. Contact information for a psychiatrist in the Ninth.

A note was scribbled on the bottom:

Jean-Louis wants you to call this doctor. He uses a brain scan technique that is innovative. Worth a try?

Crumpling the paper, Rez made to toss it. But at the last moment, he did not. Flattening the paper on the desk, he exhaled. So Jean-Louis was having Penelope do his dirty work now?

He needed to have it out with his son, once and for all. It was what a father would do. Set his boundaries. State his purpose and expectations. Teach his son through his own example.

But was his current example really the correct one?

Blowing out a breath, Rez tilted back his head and closed his eyes. He wasn't sure anymore. He'd once thought he had it all: a loving wife, a family, and a luxury jewelry empire. And yet was it all just a façade? Was the one hundred and ten percent he put into Le Beau really worth it?

The answer had stepped into his life recently. She'd literally popped out from under a plant and smiled up at him.

"Viviane…" he whispered. Just saying her name changed his mood.

CHAPTER FIFTEEN

IT WAS COMING TOGETHER! The conservatory would soon be completed. Viv had programmed a watering schedule into the computer system in the supply room. With the sprinkler system automated—provided Rez hired someone to fill the water tanks—the garden would almost take care of itself.

Of course a monthly visit from a gardener would keep it in tiptop shape...

The idea that she might make return visits to her clients was not to be ignored. It would generate more income and ensure her creations were well kept, and if any problems or questions arose she'd be able to go over them with the garden owners.

She texted a note to Harley to add that service to her price list.

Sitting on the floor, with her list of things remaining to do before her, she leaned back on her elbows and took in the glass ceiling panels. They needed a good wash. *But I am not climbing a ladder with a wash rag and vinegar spray.* A window washer must be hired.

Next on the list was to give the tile floor a scrub. And the chandelier suspended above the circle would provide a good day of cleaning. That could be automatically lowered, but she was saving it for last.

Dancing beneath that chandelier with Rez had been a dream come true. And then making love with him... Cinderella truly had stepped out of her shoes and begun a new life.

Stretching back her arms, she felt her knuckles hit the leg of an old painted table. The pale blue paint was peeling. The roses climbing the legs and dancing across the tiny front drawer were delicate and detailed. It didn't look like an antique. Had Rez mentioned his wife had liked to paint? If Colette had painted it Viv could not move it from this room, nor even think to refinish it. It would be fine tucked next to the couch.

She recalled Rez had hinted that he and his wife had been at odds before she had died. For what reason? Viv's mind raced with scenarios. She landed instantly on an affair. But what woman in her right mind would sneak behind Rez's back and have an affair? Rez was kind, funny and handsome and...

Her shoulders slumped. Well... She had been married twenty-five years. She'd loved Brian. Still did. But if she were honest, although their relationship had started out as passionate and fiery, as the years passed it had morphed into different things. Friendship. Companionship. Sometimes dislike. Yes, they'd had their fights, like any married couple. But they had always kissed and made up. Sometimes not for days, but still… And yet over the last decade she'd noticed the frequency of sex had decreased and their love had become more based on companionship than passion. She wouldn't have traded it for anything, nor even considered seeking passion elsewhere. It was simply how their love had grown.

The last years of Brian's life had broken him. He'd been in so much pain. He'd gone from a healthy, muscled man to a frail shell of his former self who'd eventually needed a wheelchair. Viv would ask if he was in pain. He'd say he was not, but his grimace had told the truth.

Tears welled in her eyes. "I wish it could have been easier for you," she whispered.

Closing her eyes, she inhaled deeply. Just a moment for memory. Loving a strong, wonderful man for twenty-five years had truly been a gift. She had been lucky. Yet luck had once again deemed it right to surprise her with another immensely talented charming man.

And she had thought she'd never have a chance at attracting a lover into her life while here in Paris…

Her phone buzzed and Viv jumped. She mined the phone from under her discarded gardening gloves. Her friend Kiara had texted.

Possible Venice job for you. Indoor garden. Needs everything. Fast. Owner selling. Interested?

Did she even have to ask?
Viv texted back an enthusiastic yes.

Viv teased her fork through the olive oil bubbles in the balsamic vinegar that Rez had taught her was the best for dipping torn pieces of baguette. She'd wandered by a shop selling roasted chickens and the smell had decided her on a simple evening meal. Chicken, steamed *haricots verts* and bread. And lots of wine.

If someone squinted when they were looking at her they might think she was turning into a real Parisian. *Ha!* Her love language had certainly gotten a workout lately. Because, yes, she was falling for Rezin Ricard. Now, how to be sure the ghost of his wife wouldn't interfere in him seeking his own happiness…?

She set her fork aside and sipped the wine—Rez's favorite. "Is it okay if I ask you a few things about your marriage?"

He chewed slowly, then nodded. "It is fair. We are…in something here." His smile hinted at their sensual secrets. "You want to know what I am like in a relationship?"

"Maybe. Sort of. Well… We both have pasts. I can honestly say I was happily married. Brian and I were friends first, lovers second. And I can also say that I don't feel as though I'm cheating on him, or his memory, by having this relationship with you. Life goes on. We move forward."

"We do. Some faster than others. But I am at about your speed."

She smiled at that. He was still a few steps behind her. "What was your relationship with your wife like? You said she was a model? Did she travel? Were you together all the time?"

Rez leaned back in his chair, settling with a sigh. She sensed his reluctance, but also a slow percolation regarding his need to speak. The man was reactionary, but he'd learned to check his anger around her. Something she appreciated.

"She did travel a lot for her work," he said. "But the last decade she wasn't modeling often. I have always worked out of the office on the Champs-Élysées. But I traveled at least once a month to see clients or to go diamond-buying with Jean-Louis. Colette and I were friends and lovers. We were..." He blew out a breath. "Perhaps not so close the last few years. Not enemies. Only the usual marital arguments. It was just..."

Wincing inside, Viv wondered if she should have tabled her question. "It's okay," she said. "I shouldn't be nosey."

"I want to be honest with you, Viviane. But I have not said this to anyone. Ever."

She waited.

He studied his hand on the table. And then, "I

believe Colette was having *une liaison*. It was never confirmed. But the…er…intimacy between the two of us had changed enough to make me suspect. I'm not sure I ever asked her."

"You're not sure?"

He shrugged. "One of the things my memory has locked away from me…"

"Oh. I understand."

If the accident had messed with his memory, then she suspected it was the worst things to recall that might have been locked away. Who would want to remember his wife was being unfaithful to him? On the other hand, wouldn't he like to know?

That must be the reason he still couldn't let go of Colette. Not completely. He had unanswered questions.

"I am a faithful man," he said, leaning forward on his elbows. "If you choose to remain in my life I will treat you with respect and never look at another."

"If I choose?"

"Everyone has a choice about who they keep in their life, Viv."

"I'm here. Right now." She lifted her goblet in a toast.

But he didn't answer by lifting his glass. "Right now. But when the garden is complete? What next?"

He wanted to know the answer to the very

question she was trying to get answered. So the best she could give him was the truth. "A friend texted me this morning. She's a Realtor…selling a home in Venice. It's got an empty conservatory that needs a complete makeover."

"Venice is a beautiful city. Are you going to take the job?"

It was what she wanted. It was the next step in her plan to making this job work for her. But if Rez asked her to stay she knew that she would.

"I'd like to. I have a few days to make up my mind. I never make a step without thinking it through completely."

Now he lifted his goblet. "Did you think it through about me? I recall you plunged right into a kiss."

Yes, and what a plunge… No regrets. No matter how things turned out.

Really, Viv?

Fine. She would have some regrets!

"You are my leap," she finally said.

"How did that go?"

"I'm still falling." Viv smiled at him over another sip of wine.

"I'll catch you. Promise."

"I know that you will."

And he'd do it without stepping on her memories. She should show him the same respect. Whatever he'd had with Colette, she would let it be. It wasn't her place to butt in.

"So how was your day at work? You mentioned you're designing something for that prince?"

"A wedding set. It's a study in attempting to take his horrendously blingy idea and make it classy. But I won't tell him that. He'll be happy with the final product."

"Who wouldn't? To have Rezin Ricard design your wedding set? What a dream!"

"You sound like a fan."

"I wore that diamond necklace. I think I've dreamt about it since. I've never been a diamond girl, but that big pink stone changed my mind."

"It's good to be flexible. And…"

He heaved out a sigh and Viv sensed their flirtation had ended.

"And I've been flexible today, too. I made an appointment to see a psychiatrist that Jean-Louis selected."

"Oh, Rez, how does that make you feel?"

"Honestly? I'm trying not to be so rigid. Maybe this doc will have something new to say. Apparently he utilizes a brain scan and has a unique rehabilitation program."

"Sounds encouraging."

Rez reached for her hand and kissed it. "There's one thing, though."

She clasped her hand over theirs. "Yes?"

"I'm…apprehensive about the appointment. I have such awful memories of the weeks and months following the accident. Of those horrible days spent in the hospital, interacting with doctors when my brain was not functioning at top performance. So I'm…nervous." He rubbed his jaw. "Would you…come along with me?"

"Of course I will."

He'd asked for help. Viv would gladly be there with a hand to his back again.

CHAPTER SIXTEEN

AN HOUR LATER, they'd finished off the bottle of wine and pulled on their clothes after impromptu sex in the garden. There was just something about that sexy velvet piece of furniture... Now they snuggled there on the sofa, wrapped in the blanket, heads tilted back to take in the Parisian night.

Rez brushed the hair from Viv's face. "I like it when you're mussed."

"That's my go-to look. I work hard to achieve such disarray."

She laughed and tucked her head against his shoulder. It had been a while since she had laughed so freely. Forgotten her woes and the insistent need to work for a meager wage simply to exist. Life had taken a drastic turn because she had dared to dive in. She never wanted to surface.

"I like what you've done in here. It looks completely different. You're a nurturer, Viv."

"I've never been called that before, but I'll take it. You didn't have too many dead plants in here, but so many were stretching toward the light. I had to prune them back. If you hire a gardener to come in once a month and check in on things, it should stay in shape."

"I'll add that to my list. Or I could hire you?"

"I have decided to add that to my *à la carte* list. Return visits."

"Sign me up. That is, if you'll be in the city."

She met his gaze and knew exactly what he was thinking about. The long-distance relationship thing. Probably wouldn't work out. Maybe it would? But there were ways to make it easier for the two of them. If they both agreed they wanted to continue with this relationship.

"I'll go where the jobs take me," she said. "But I may also consider where my heart wishes me to land. Although Paris is out of the question, rent-wise."

"If you charge your clients appropriately you'll be able to afford a *pied-à-terre* in no time."

No mention of her staying with him. Had she expected him to make that offer? She wasn't sure. It felt fast. And yet they felt so right.

"You saved that wobbly little table?" Rez asked.

"Yes, it's pretty." She stood and picked up the table. Setting it beside the sofa, she tapped the crackled paint. "Did your wife paint it?"

"I'm not sure. Possibly? Those do resemble roses."

"Oh, yes—probably those roses in the corner that I absolutely have not touched."

He smirked. "It's a good business model to do as the client requests."

He pulled the table closer, and one of the legs caught on a floor tile. The table toppled. Rez swore and lunged to catch it, but wasn't fast enough. The drawer jarred open and out spilled a cell phone. One of the older flip-type models. Viv had seen them for sale at the tourist shops. Cheap and disposable.

"What the…?" Rez picked up the phone.

Had the phone belonged to Colette? It did not look like a phone such a woman would have been seen touching. It probably didn't even have a color screen. It must belong to someone else. Maybe a maid, or someone who had tended the garden before it had been forgotten and left to grow wild?

Suddenly Rez's face tightened, his jaw pulsing as he studied the item. Did he recognize it as Colette's? It could mean something terrible. Or it could be nothing more than a spare phone.

Rez hissed something in French and pressed the phone against his chest. Viv took the statement to be meaningful, for he'd closed his eyes in reverence.

"I…uh…" She didn't know what to do right now. A hand against his back didn't feel right.

"I will need to be alone." Rez stood and marched out of the garden, taking the phone along with him.

Viv swallowed. What had just happened? Was

the phone Colette's? He had mentioned something about believing his wife had an affair. Oh, heck. Things had just gone south.

Rez limped into the bedroom, kicking the door closed behind him. He made it to the bed. Dropping the cell phone, he fell to his knees before the mattress and bowed his head.

Memory flooded his brain. He and Colette in the car that fateful night. They had been arguing... Rain had been beating the car's exterior... Colette had been an excellent driver, and she'd slowed on the dark country road as they'd journeyed back to Paris from Vaux-le-Vicomte, where they'd attended a dinner hosted by one of his clients. Rez, ever the one who needed to be in control, had clutched the armrest to keep himself from asking if he should drive. They would be fine. He trusted Colette's driving.

But he hadn't trusted *her*.

Not after what he had found...

"How's the garden?" he'd asked tightly.

Colette flashed a glance at him. Pursed her lips. Focused on the road. "It's lovely, *mon cher*. As always. Why do you ask?"

"Just thinking about...gardens." The rain pounded the windows.

"You never ask about the mansion...what I do there. I am surprised you care."

"It's your *tanière*. Whatever you've asked from

me, I've given to you. I've respected your need to have an escape from me."

"Rezin! It is not an escape from you. You know I like to paint and garden. I do not desire escape—ever. I live for socializing. Why do you think I look forward to the occasional dinner party so much?"

"You were distracted the entire night," he stated through a tense jaw.

He'd heard the phone call earlier, when Colette had slipped away from the outdoor party and moved behind a hedgerow. He never jumped to conclusions. But she'd been gone longer than felt right.

Before he could stop himself, he asked, "Are you having a liaison?"

"What?" She looked to him.

He gestured to her to keep her attention on the road. She gripped the steering wheel. Her entire profile tightened.

"I heard you on the phone."

He looked away from her. The rain began to dissipate. *Merci à Dieu.*

"Kissing." It had been the sound of an air-kiss. But no simple kiss of greeting had ever been accompanied by a sultry moan.

"Rez."

"I *heard*, Colette."

She pouted. He didn't expect to see tears. She wasn't that kind of drama queen. Always in control. Always sure of everything she felt she was owed, deserved, or had earned.

When she shrugged, Rez's heart took a dive. He crushed his eyelids tightly shut.

"Well," she started, in the light tone that she assumed when she tried to believe her own lies, "it is what all Frenchwomen do. *Oui?* It is nothing, Rezin. A folly."

"Nothing?"

His heart pounded his ribcage, confirming what he'd not wanted to be confirmed after finding the phone in the little table she kept in her garden when he'd gone looking for her. She had been unfaithful. After thirty years of marriage. Or had it been longer than that? *Merde.*

"Unless you are in an eighteenth-century costume drama, it is not 'nothing,' Colette. All Frenchwomen? Is that your excuse? I thought you loved me?"

"I do! I just require—change. You know?"

Yes, she liked to change—her hairstyle, her fashion choices, the colors on the walls and even her breasts. But love? His love for Colette had been unwavering.

"Our love has gotten…" she searched for the word "…quieter. I wanted to find the fire again. Something louder."

Louder? What the hell was she talking about? It was bad enough that his heart was cleaving in two.

The car swerved.

Rez reached for the wheel.

Bright lights from an oncoming car blinded him.

Colette twisted the wheel and screamed.

The wheels barreled over rough terrain. A forest paralleled one side of them. He couldn't be sure which way they had gone off course. But the other car had not hit them. *Whew!*

Just when Rez felt he might gain control of the wheel, the world had jerked to a halt. Colette's scream was the last sound he heard before the windshield shattered. Then an excruciating pain cut through his leg. He blacked out.

Now, Rez clenched the counterpane. This was the first time he'd remembered that night since coming round in the hospital. Remembered that moment when the fight had culminated and Colette had lost control of the vehicle.

The crash replayed in slow motion in his memory. In reality, it had probably been two seconds from the car going off the road to the front end hitting a boulder and flipping over, only to be literally speared by a tree. The thick branch had pushed through the car's metal frame—and Rez's left leg. He'd been pinned inside the vehicle.

Colette, who had not been wearing a seatbelt, had been thrown through the windshield, her body slammed onto a bed of boulders. The doctors had told him she had died instantly from massive head trauma.

He crushed the cell phone in his grip.

He'd thought to move forward. Come to terms with the cruel trick life had played on him. And yet *he* was to blame for the accident. He should have died, too.

Rez slammed the phone onto the floor. The hard plastic shell didn't break. He swore, and kicked the thing across the floor. It wedged under the closed door.

Pressing his thumb under his brow, he closed his eyes, cautioning himself against the dizzy spell that threatened. It was not something he could control. Slapping his hands to the floor, he felt the world begin to spin, very much as it had in the car with Colette...

CHAPTER SEVENTEEN

REZ CAME TO on the floor. He'd not fallen asleep. A dizzy spell had knocked him flat. A bad one this time.

He sat up and swore. Then looked around to make sure no one had witnessed his collapse. Immediately following the accident he'd gone down like that about once or twice every few months. His doctor had suggested it was a condition of his brain injury and that he would have to learn to live with it.

He *was* living with it. It wasn't that he was incapable. He simply had moments when his body didn't want to be upright. So he went horizontal. A few moments later he got up and went on with life. But try explaining that to a son who wanted to send his father to a psychiatrist. Though he knew Jean-Louis was only showing concern. And perhaps his son wasn't so desperate to toss out his father and sit in the CEO's chair.

Leaning his elbows on the bed, he caught his head in his hands. Was he being too adamant in refusing Jean-Louis's desire to jump in and handle the company? Should his son not be allowed to make some mistakes while he learned? Rez had been younger than Jean-Louis when he had taken over—in his twenties. Of course Jean-Louis could do the job. It was just the designing of jewelry that was Rez's life's work. It gave him joy. It was his *raison d'être*.

At the very least he'd made a concession with the psychiatrist appointment. He expected little from it. But perhaps Jean-Louis would see he was trying.

Wandering into the bathroom, he flicked on the faucet. Leaning over the sink, he splashed his face with cold water.

Back in the bedroom he noticed the phone on the floor. Incredible that something so small had been the catalyst for a devastating memory. Colette had been unfaithful to him. And that phone was proof of it. Could it have been with her security guard, Boris? Likely. But he had no desire to charge it to see whom she had called or how often.

He left it there, disgusted with his reaction to it.

Heading down the stairs and into the kitchen, he glanced toward the conservatory. The door was open. Was Viv in there?

He slammed down a couple electrolyte tablets and grabbed a bottle of water from the fridge. He couldn't hide from Viv. He didn't want to. Going to her felt…not desperate, but rather like seeking solace. And yet what would he tell Viv now? That he had distracted his wife so that the accident had happened? Had taken her life and destroyed his, as well as his son's? Perhaps he did need to lie on a psychiatrist's couch and have his brain examined.

Rez wandered through the foyer to the open garden doors. Viv was not inside. He took in the newly ordered foliage with a changed perspective. Viv's handiwork had breathed life into Colette's ghost. Viv's husband haunted her with music; Colette haunted Rez with this garden.

He glanced to the overhead windows, scanning across the curved roof until he spied the cracked glass. He'd have to call in a glazier to take care of that. And to check the rest of the panes, to ensure no others were in need of repair. He must maintain the value of this house. Because it was time to let it go. To finally sweep away Colette's memory. Or rather, to tuck it away. He couldn't excise her from his heart. She was Jean-Louis's mother.

Rez sighed, shoved his hands in his pockets, and wandered over to the roses. There were no blooms, and they were overgrown and ugly. He remembered Colette bringing home a bouquet after a weekend retreat here. The frothy blooms had perfumed the bedroom. It was a scent he'd never cared for, but it had made Colette purr in delight. Because they reminded her of chats with her lover? *Had* it been the security guard as he'd suspected?

Swearing, Rez gripped a branch. He wrenched at it, uprooting it from the dry earth. Tossing it aside, he grabbed another branch. Yanked and tossed. Anger seethed from his pores. All French-women took lovers. That was what Colette had said. As if she had expected he wouldn't mind her infidelity.

A thorn ripped his palm. Rez swore again and pulled harder, unearthing a whole plant and tossing it aside. A scatter of brown stalks lay around him. Dirt dusted his shoes. His hands bled. He hadn't felt the thorns. The pain in his heart was the only thing that tortured him now.

"Rez? I heard you shout— Oh." Viv raced over to him and grabbed his hands. "Oh, no, Rez…"

He tugged away from her and stepped back, putting up a palm for distance. "She had a liaison. She told me that night of the accident. *Merde!*"

He stepped over to the sofa and let his body land, elbows catching on his knees. When Viviane disappeared for a few moments he immediately wanted her back. By his side.

Don't abandon me. You are my breath now.

And then she kneeled before him, a wet towel in her hands. She dabbed at his palms, her touch gentle but firm. He bowed his head to hers. Safe with her. Loved.

"I'd suspected for a while," he whispered. "We fought. The argument distracted her. She lost control of the car and it veered off the road. It was my fault."

"No," Viv insisted softly. "You couldn't have known what would happen."

"I tried to get hold of the steering wheel."

"You did. You're a good man, Rez. It was an accident."

Viv kissed his palm. He didn't know what he had done to deserve this woman in his life. She was good. Perhaps too good for him. Would he make her want to seek attention elsewhere as he had with Colette?

"The phone jarred my memory." He blew out a breath. "You are too kind to me, Viviane."

"I care about you." Taking both his hands in hers, she gently kissed the knuckles, then turned them to study the cuts. "Just some minor cuts. But I should see if you have some antiseptic."

"Do you have gloves?"

"No... I suppose I should have thought about being sterile—"

"Gardening gloves. I'm not leaving this room until those roses are gone."

"Oh." She nodded. "There are some in the supply room. A couple pairs. I'll help you!" she called as she wandered to the back of the conservatory.

Rez studied his bleeding palms. It was a small price to pay for unearthing a haunting pain.

Viv kissed Rez's shoulder, then down his bare back. No freckles that she could find. And when she touched the scar on his leg he allowed it. They had made love. Now their bodies were lax and perspiring. A full moon shone across the bed. The twinkling Eiffel Tower had become their voyeur.

Yet she wasn't troubled by Rez's quietness. Poor man. He'd just remembered his wife had had an affair. Colette was no longer in the picture, and it might seem as though it shouldn't matter anymore. But Viv wasn't stupid. It mattered. Could this new knowledge derail their future? What *was* their future?

"You okay?" she asked.

"I am when I make love with you."

"Me too. But I mean about…you know…earlier. Remembering things."

He turned onto his back and she nestled her head on his chest, where dark hairs tickled her cheek.

"I've felt there was something I was missing," he said. "Something dark. Now I know what that was. It's big, but also I feel relief. Does that sound strange to you?"

"If it's how you feel, then it's your truth." She kissed his chest, then rested her chin on her hand to look at him. "I have to say something, but I don't want you to think I'm saying it to manipulate you or gloss over your pain."

"What is it?"

"I care about you. I love you. You've come to mean the world to me. And when you're hurt, it hurts my heart as well."

"Thank you. And you mean so much to me. It feels as though you are in my life for a reason. You understand me. It's easy to be with you."

"Same."

He hadn't said he loved her. Selfish of her to expect such a confession after what he'd just remembered about his wife.

"You're changing me, Viv."

"Is that good, bad, or strange?"

He chuckled. "Kind of...sort of...good."

Viv stared up at the giant crystal chandelier. It looked as though a century of dust had gathered on the elaborate structure. Dusting and cleaning it would take a good day.

Rez hadn't said he loved her. Would he ever? Or was there no future for them? Had she jumped in too deep? Maybe it was time to step back, take a wider view and see what she'd really gotten into. If it was anything at all. The man was obviously haunted by his wife and her indiscretions. Was it too late to pull some armor around her heart?

"Viviane!"

Startled by the familiar female voice, Viv spun

and caught her best friend in her arms. "Kiara? What—? I…"

Heck, she hadn't seen Kiara in person for over a year. Viv tightened the hug and lifted her friend and spun her around.

When they parted, Kiara held out Viv's arms. "You look so good. The Paris air certainly does you well. Your cheeks glow. And look at your hair! It's grown half a foot since we last saw one another."

"Well, you look the same. Slim, tanned, sexy, put together, and worth a million bucks."

Kiara waggled her shoulders proudly. "That's around five million now. I just sold a chateau west of Caen to the former NHL player Bear Bradford. My commission was insane."

"Oh, my God. We need to gossip. I want to hear it all. But why are you here? I don't understand."

"Didn't your lover boy tell you? He's put this place up for sale. He wants me to sell it. I was in Marseilles, working another sale, so I flew in immediately. It seemed urgent."

"It did?"

"Yes."

Kiara didn't pick up on Viv's annoyance as she strode across the tiled floor. She'd always been a fan of a body-hugging dress, and the bright red of the one she wore was her color. And those shoes had red heels. She really was living the dream.

"Look what you've done to this garden!" Kiara

exclaimed. "I saw the 'before' photos of it. This is going to be a huge selling point. Besides the fact this is a fabulous mansion set riverside in Paris. Oh, Viv!"

Viviane couldn't find the same enthusiasm as her friend.

Rez had put the mansion up for sale? But she wasn't finished with the garden's refurbishment. And—and why would he sell such a lovely property? Didn't his son use it? And his mother-in-law? Had it something to do with him remembering his wife's affair?

Viv clasped a hand over her thudding heart. Pulling up the rose bushes hadn't been enough for him. He must have decided to excise Colette's ghost in the most extreme manner possible. And in the process would he also excise Viv from his life?

"What's going on in your brain?" Kiara twirled a finger before Viv's face. "You don't look happy, sweetie. Did I say something wrong? You didn't know about the sale?"

Viv shook her head. "I need to talk to Rez about this."

She started toward the doors. But then she remembered that her friend, whom she hadn't seen in forever, was here, and they needed to do girlfriend things…and chat…and…

"I won't be long! You have some things to do, yes?"

Kiara shrugged. "Yes, I need to go through the whole place. Should take the afternoon."

"Great. Help yourself to food in the kitchen. We can go out to eat later and catch up."

"You sure you're all right?"

"I'm not sure. That's why I need to talk to Rez. I'll be back soon. I'm so glad you're here!"

"I fly out tonight, so…" Kiara snapped her fingers. "Make it quick."

"I will!"

CHAPTER EIGHTEEN

PENELOPE, LE BEAU'S perky red-headed reception-ist, with apple cheeks and long lashes, remembered Viv from the party. When she explained that Rez had left early because his penthouse was finished, she happily provided Viv with the address.

He'd not told her that his home was finished. Penelope had made it sound as though it had been for days. So why had he still been living at the mansion?

Where was Rez's head lately? Had it to do with his injury? His crash into memory after discovering the phone? Now she was really worried about him.

Unless...

Unless he was purposely avoiding her. He had good reason to. There was the whole learning about his wife having an affair thing—but still... That had nothing to do with Viviane. Had he suddenly decided he didn't want a relationship with her?

Speed-walking across a bridge to the Left Bank, Viviane wandered the streets in the Sixth Arrondissement, using the small guidebook that she'd picked up at a bookstore during one of her morning jaunts. The Saint-Germain-des-Prés neighborhood was old money, or so the guidebook stated. The tourist-crowded streets were lined with art galleries, restaurants, mature trees, and brick-fronted buildings.

The front of Rez's building boasted a gorgeous iridescent-tiled design, highlighted here and there with deep indigo tiles. A little modern, a touch Moroccan, it reminded her of the conservatory floor. When she pressed the bell for the top floor, Rez immediately buzzed her in without asking who it was. He stood in the open doorway, waiting, as she topped the stairs.

"Were you expecting me?" she asked as she walked toward him.

"Yes and no. I suspect Mademoiselle Kirk has arrived at the mansion?"

"She has." She stopped before him, taking him in. No shoes, a loose pair of faded jeans. Casual black tee shirt and tousled hair. He looked so un-businesslike, and not at all the image of the CEO of a billion-dollar jewelry company. "Are you okay?"

"Come inside."

That wasn't an answer.

Steeling herself for some heavy insight into Rez's memory vault, Viv crossed the threshold. The penthouse was airy and bright, with high ceilings and a glass roof that curved up from the wall and halfway across the ceiling. The walls were brick and rough timber. The floors wide herringbone. And everywhere there was leather furniture and black metal touches. A total man cave, but with the elan of taste.

"They knocked out a wall here," Rez said as he wandered into the kitchen and grabbed a bottle of wine. "It is nice to have the entire area open now."

"It's gorgeous. Modern. Exactly what I expected your style to be."

"Not like some centuries-old mansion?" He handed her the bottle. "Sip?"

Had he been drinking all morning? Or was he employing the "sip" plan to avoid discussion? She wasn't in the mood to pussyfoot around the difficult stuff today.

"Rez, why didn't you tell me your penthouse was complete? That…that you're staying here again?"

"I…uh…sorry. I just needed a place to sort my thoughts today. It wasn't meant to be disrespectful to you."

"Oh. Well, I can appreciate that. Of course you need some space."

"I do—"

"But you can't sell the mansion. It means something to you. And doesn't your son have memories there?"

"So we're going right there? I should expect

nothing less from you." He countered that with a brief smile. "Viv, when I found that phone I remembered the one thing that should have stayed forgotten."

"I'm so sorry."

"It's too much, Viviane. I can't keep that place anymore. I need to move on."

Though she wanted to argue, she knew she didn't have any right to question Rez's relationship with his wife. Or what he did to try to erase those memories. But it still didn't feel right to get rid of such a beautiful home. A home his mother-in-law surely loved. Did Coral know about her daughter's infidelity?

But, even more so, Viv wasn't ready to give up on her dream.

"I'm not finished with the garden," she said quietly.

"You'll finish. You said you'd only a few days remaining?"

"Yes. But Kiara said the mansion would go in a day."

"Most likely. She's a hot seller. But it'll take time to—what do they call it?—stage the place?"

Viviane sighed. Maybe a day at the most. That mansion was perfection. Save for the garden—which, if she hurried, could be viewer-ready in a few days. The final photos wouldn't be nearly as perfect as she'd hoped, though.

Heck, this wasn't cataclysmic to her dream. It

was just a little setback. She should not overreact. Yet it felt deeper. Like an attack on her very being. When she had done nothing wrong!

"I'm sorry, Rez."

"Thank you. Now…" His heavy sigh did not warrant good news. "I still need some space today. Please…?"

Yikes. He didn't want her around. This was bigger than a setback.

"Sure, I get it."

Not completely. Don't push me away!

"I want to spend some time with Kiara before she has to fly out," she told him. "Can I pick up something for you to eat and drop it off?"

"No, I'm fine." He wandered toward the windows, hands in his pockets, back to her.

He was not fine. But it did not feel like her place to step in and try to make things better. Something held Viv back from taking a firm stance about being there for him. Could it be the ghost of his cheating wife? Could Rez ever trust another woman?

Oh, this was not good.

"I'll see you tomorrow, then. Stop by or give me a call." She walked to the door, waiting for his response, but he didn't give her one.

Viv left with her heart pounding and tears rolling down her cheeks. The man was hurting. And she'd done everything she could to help with that.

Now it was up to him, and things would happen at his own pace.

Unfortunately, that pace didn't mesh with hers. Or the time she'd allotted for staying in Paris. If she were to move forward with her dream job that meant moving on to another client, perhaps in another country. Far from Rez. They didn't have the luxury right now to take a day away from one another. They really needed to get straight what their intentions for this relationship were. If they even wanted to remain a couple now, with this new information about his wife.

But she would never force him. This was more than grief; it was anger and betrayal. So she must be patient.

Once back at the mansion, Viv deposited the cheese, baguettes and sliced meats she'd picked up along the way onto the counter. Pouring two goblets of wine, she then went in search of her friend.

"Kiara!"

"Behind you!"

Viv spun, and her friend rushed to catch one goblet before wine sloshed over the rim.

"I was in the library," Kiara said, and sipped. "Ooh, this is nice. You've never been a big wine drinker before."

Viv shrugged. "It's the new me. Rez introduced me to this stuff and I can't get enough."

"I like the new you. She's still as beautiful

and smart as the old Viv, but this version..." Kiara made a show of looking her up and down "...seems more frisky. Open."

"Sweetie, I've taken a French lover," Viv said with aplomb. Though it felt forced. "That's about as frisky as it gets."

Kiara hooked an arm in Viv's and steered her toward the conservatory. "Tell me everything. My flight doesn't leave until nine, so we've got time."

Hours later, after gossip, girl confessions, and unabashed consumption of meats and cheese, the two women sat on the sofa, heads back and legs stretched out. Kiara's Louboutins sat on the floor, discarded for comfort.

Viviane felt no jealousy at all when comparing them with her chinos, blouse and sandals. She had something that made her feel like she owned the world.

"Rez is perfect, Kiara. But there's the long-distance thing I worry about. And, well, should I even try to make it work?"

Kiara sat up abruptly and gave her a discerning onceover. "Why would you think otherwise?"

Yes—why? Was she already making up reasons not to fall to pieces should she and Rez not work out? Forming a protective armor about her heart? Possibly.

"Kiara, I've been out of the dating loop for over twenty-five years. I did find a keeper, but...

I don't know. Maybe I should play the field? See what else is out there."

"Seriously? Do you *want* to do that?"

No, no, and definitely no. Only a fool would walk away from a man who felt like a perfect match. As close to perfect as could happen.

Viv sighed. "Dating *is* a lot of work. And I do love Rez."

"Then that's your answer."

"But does he love me? He's having a tough go of it right now. I'm not so sure I landed in his life at the right time for him to start over. I thought we were really connecting, but then his grief punched him with some awful memories. Selling this place is a reaction to that. I don't think he should sell. It means something to his family. But he's only just remembered that his wife had an affair and that's why he's getting rid of this place—because it used to be hers."

"Viv, dear, why do you need him to keep it?"

Interesting question. Why, indeed? She had no right to influence Rez's personal decisions. And this place *had* been his cheating wife's hideaway.

On the other hand… "His son uses it. And his mother-in-law. There must be a good reason Coral wanted the garden refurbished. In memory of her daughter?"

"Yes, that was her intention," Kiara said thoughtfully.

"If Rez can't be here, he should at least allow his family to enjoy the place."

"You mustn't convince him to keep it," Kiara pleaded.

"Why not?"

"Because then I'll lose a huge commission!"

"I'm sorry. It's...complicated."

Kiara tilted her head onto Viv's shoulder. They shared the blanket between them.

"Is it hard to move on after being married to Brian for so long?"

"Yes, and no. I mean, I don't feel guilty. But I'm not sure if I should feel guilty for *not* feeling guilty. Brian is gone. Longing for him to be alive or continuing to mourn is not going to bring him back. I'm ready, Kiara. And it feels damn good to have the attention of another man. Rez makes me feel sexy. And you know I would never call myself old—fifty is the new thirty, don't you know?— but I really do love the attention."

"You are not old. I can only hope to have such luminous skin and hair when I'm your age."

"When you're *my* age? Don't make me sound decrepit, Kiara. You're turning forty this year."

"Ixnay on the ortyfay. I intend to remain eternally thirty-nine."

"Join the club."

Her friend tilted the last drops of wine into their glasses, then tapped the air with the empty bottle. "Here's to love! Be it true, new, or rocky."

"You're toasting love? Well, well, well… That makes me wonder if you have a new boyfriend!"

Kiara sighed. "Too busy. All I can manage is a hookup here and there. Benetto in Naples is a dream. We eat. We have sex. I can slip out in the morning without having a conversation. It's optimal."

"You've *never* been so poor on relationships. What's up?"

"Like I said. I'm too busy. And…well, you know… What does a relationship really have to offer me?"

Kiara had found out a few years earlier that she wasn't able to have children. She had always wanted a big family with lots of kids. Viv remembered that evening how her friend had cried over the devastating news, and how she'd moved out of her boyfriend's home that same evening, never to see him again. Kiara hadn't the heart to tell him the truth about their split. It was an extremely touchy subject for Kiara.

As for what a relationship could offer a woman…?

"Good sex?" she tried.

"Most of the time it's good," Kiara agreed. "So how is it with Rezin? I love that name. And he is so sexy. Tall, dark, and handsome. And a millionaire?"

"Billionaire."

"Nice! You found the perfect man."

"I was thinking much the same. Now? How to keep him?"

The twosome laughed and finished their wine before calling Kiara a cab for the airport.

CHAPTER NINETEEN

TRACKING A MORNING beam of sunshine through the garden to the supply room, Viv flicked the switch to move the chandelier. The electronic mechanism slowly lowered the heavy extravagance until the bottommost crystal dangled about six inches from the ground. Washcloths, a lemon and vinegar solution, and bucket of warm water for cleaning it sat ready. The dust was thick, and a fingernail test determined it was caked on as hard as paint.

This was going to require elbow grease.

"Should have gone for a walk first," she muttered as she circled the huge creation, deciding where to begin. She'd take a break after a few hours, and head out for coffee and a pastry.

It had been sad to wake in bed alone. Rez hadn't texted or called.

But Viv would not dwell on his absence. Not for a while, at least. She figured she could distract herself from worrying about their relationship for at least an hour or two with intense cleaning. After that, all bets were off.

She bent to retrieve a dusting cloth, and when

she stood bumped into the chandelier. It wobbled. The sound of something cracking alerted her. Had she broken a crystal?

When a sudden slice of heat seared her shoulder she let out a yelp and grabbed her shoulder. Her fingers came away with blood on them. Viviane winced at the pain. She stepped away from the chandelier and saw shattered glass on the floor. Those thin shards could have only come from…

She looked up. The cracked glass pane had fallen out. Another small triangle of glass dangled from the iron frame. It could fall at any moment.

She jumped back—and into the arms of Rez. Spinning to face him, she let out another yelp.

"Viv, I heard you scream. What the—? You're bleeding."

"I didn't scream. It was a minor outburst."

"Why are you bleeding? Did you cut yourself on the chandelier?"

"No, the broken ceiling glass fell. I think it got joggled loose when I bumped the chandelier." She tapped her shoulder. "Is it bad?"

He swore as he pushed up the back of her tee shirt to study the damage. "There's a lot of blood. You don't feel that? It could be deep. I'll call SOS Médecins."

"SOS?"

"They do house calls. Faster than the emergency room. On the other hand…" He swore again. "I don't know. The ER might have the best equipment to deal with this if it *is* serious."

"Hospitals freak me out. What are you doing here, anyway? Maybe some iodine and I'll be fine."

"Henri is waiting out front," he said urgently. "He can get us there quickly. Is that the only place you were hurt? Are you okay? Viv?"

The last thing she heard was her name. Then the world went black.

Rez paced beside the emergency room bed on which Viviane lay. He'd carried her to the car following her faint in the conservatory. The physician here had foregone stitches. The long surface cut had just required taping shut with skin closure strips. Viv would be fine, but they would not release her until the doctor on call signed her off. She dozed right now, in and out of sleep. The chemist had provided a pill to relax her while they had been prepping the wound.

This was his fault. If he'd called the glazier when he'd been thinking to do so this accident would have never happened. *Mon Dieu*, yet another woman damaged by his indifference. Colette had said the fire had left their relationship. Was this too much fire for he and Viviane?

His watch buzzed. He checked the notification. A ten a.m. meeting with the Prince. It was important he be there to finalize the wedding set design.

He knew Henri could drive him to Le Beau in less than twenty minutes if they left now. He also knew that if he were late Penelope knew where he kept the hard copy design file and could access it, hand it over to Jean-Louis.

Rez leaned over Viv. She smiled wearily and her eyelids fluttered. He kissed her forehead, her cheek, and her nose, where those six freckles danced as she wrinkled it in reaction.

"How do you feel?" he asked.

"I'll be fine." She lay on her side. The hospital gown exposed the place where the wound ran from the top of her shoulder to mid-back. "You think they'll let me wear this fancy gown home?"

"I'll have Henri bring in something for you to wear." Rez texted his driver and suggested a nearby tourist shop across the river that would provide a tee shirt. "Done."

"When can I leave?"

He shrugged. "We're waiting on the official sign-off. Just relax, Viv. I'm here with you. We have all the time in the world."

A tear rolled down her cheek.

"Viv...?"

She swiped at the tear. "Sorry. So much is going on in my life. Big, heavy stuff. I lost my husband. I'm in a foreign land. I'm starting a new job that has no guarantee it will be successful. I'm never sure if my blushes are hot flashes. I found a sexy Frenchman who actually seems to enjoy my company, but he's got a dead wife to deal with. And I'm not sure if he'll choose me over her. It's a lot."

Yes, the dead wife. Who shouldn't be in the middle of this new relationship. But, strangely, she was. And, as much as he wanted to reassure Viv who his choice would be, right now she wasn't in any frame of mind to really hear him.

"It is a lot."

"But if I'm truthful, it's actually exhilarating. Scary exhilarating."

"I'm impressed."

"By what?"

"You could have gone the victim route. *Everything is terrible and it's all happening because I don't know where I'm going or what I'm doing.* But you embrace the challenge of the new. You are a strong, confident woman, Viv."

"I am," she said with surprise. "And I'm so fortunate. I'm in Paris. I have a job for the moment. And I enjoy that job. And…well, there's you. Life is really good." She closed her eyes. "Now that I think of it, why are you here? You should be at work. You can leave me. I'll be fine."

"I know you will be." He glanced toward the hallway that led to the entrance doors. When Henri arrived with the shirt, he would make his escape to Le Beau.

Or…

He sat on the chair beside her bed. For the first

time, work was not the place he wanted to be. Kissing the back of Viv's hand, he smoothed his cheek along her soft, warm skin.

"This is where I want to be."

After being discharged from the emergency room, Viv slid with Rez into the back of the limo and Henri drove them to a Lebanese restaurant in the Fifth, at Rez's direction. Nestled amidst a forest of ferns and a babbling brook, they enjoyed mezze, tea, and some exotic music.

That really hit the spot. Viv had been famished. Now she felt better—if a little tired from the morning's adventure. Her new tee shirt featured a black cat with a red beret forming a smooch with its mouth. That Henri…such a joker.

"Did you take the day off to spend it with me?" she asked as they walked through the courtyard toward the mansion entrance.

"You got a problem with that?"

"Not at all. But you're thinking about work."

"I am not." He punched in the digital code and allowed her inside before him. "I called a glazier while they were fixing you up. He should be here within the hour, to fix the glass and check the entire ceiling. No working on the chandelier until he gives you the A-OK."

"Deal. I can do some groundwork the rest of the day."

"Absolutely not." Rez took Viv in his arms. "I took the day off. We're going to spend it together. Nothing fancy…just a nice afternoon enjoying one another's company."

"Nestled on the sofa in the garden?"

"I like the sound of that. Maybe some slow dancing later?"

"You do know how to romance a woman."

Before she could kiss him, he pressed a finger to her lips. "I need to apologize for my freakout, and…and for selling the mansion. Things are tough right now. Jean-Louis is putting pressure on me. And remembering about Colette's infidelities really threw me. It was a reaction. Poorly thought out decision. But I realized one thing."

"What's that?"

Just as Rez was about to say something that she felt would be important, the mansion door swung open and in walked Jean-Louis. The man showed immediate surprise to see his father standing there with her in his arms.

Viv's discomfort manifested itself in her wiggling out of Rez's embrace.

"Papa?"

"Jean-Louis, I didn't expect you to stop by."

"I didn't expect to find you here at Maman's *tanière*. I thought the penthouse was finished? Are you…still staying here?"

Jean-Louis gave Viviane a onceover. It didn't

feel like he was giving her a glowing assessment, either.

He said something in French, and Rez answered in French. It all went over Viv's head. But she did sense she was not being welcomed into this conversation. At least, not by Jean-Louis.

She stepped back, walking toward the conservatory. "I'll leave you two to talk." She gave a sheepish wave, but neither paid her any mind as they continued their discussion in rising tones and in heated French.

What she wouldn't give to understand the language. But she suspected this was the showdown Rez had dreaded.

"So she is more than just a gardener," Jean-Louis stated.

Rez had sensed Viviane backing away and leaving them. He'd almost called for her to stay, but then they'd have to speak English, and he knew Jean-Louis would scoff at that.

"Papa!"

"She's my..." Rez almost said *lover*, but the term didn't feel right for this moment. He had intended to formally introduce Viviane as his significant other to his son. Not blurt it out in the middle of an argument. "I care about her, Jean-Louis. She means something to me."

Jean-Louis thrust out an arm as he scoffed, "So

that is why you missed the meeting this morning? You were in bed with your lover?"

"Watch it," Rez warned. His son had no right to speak to him in such a manner. "You may believe I am an invalid, but I still command respect as your father."

"Dad, you missed an important meeting."

"I am aware of that."

Jean-Louis's mouth dropped open.

"I saw the reminder. But when I got it I was in the emergency room with Viv. A glass panel from the conservatory fell and cut her."

"Is she okay?"

Rez knew Jean-Louis was not cruel; he simply had a focus that would eventually prove him a force at Le Beau.

Much like his father.

And just now Rez had realized he could let go. At least some of it.

"She'll be fine. It was a long cut, but not deep. It was a good thing I did allow her to refurbish the garden. The plants had taken over, and had she not cut down most of them more than one panel may have dropped out. The entire roof could have collapsed."

"It is good to know the room has been spared. It was special to Maman. She would want the garden to be kept vital."

Rez would never tell Jean-Louis that Colette

had been unfaithful. It wasn't fair when his son had no means to go to his mother to confirm such an accusation. And he would not speak ill of the dead. Jean-Louis deserved to hold his mother in high esteem.

"The Prince is pleased with the design," Jean-Louis said. "You should have been there to see the smile on his face."

"I'm sorry. I could have been there. But I… I made a choice."

"And that choice was the American woman?"

He met his son's eyes and tried to show him his sincerity. His genuine need to simply be understood by him. As Viv understood him. That was the most intimate thing he could imagine between two people: an innate understanding. All he asked of Jean-Louis was that he not judge him. That he allowed him to walk through his life and make his mistakes and learn as he went.

But his son suffered, too. And sometimes Rez forgot that.

"How are you, Jean-Louis?"

His son tilted his gaze down. His shoulders slumped.

"I don't ask enough. We're both so busy with work. We tend to act more as office mates than father and son at times. That's wrong. And I'm so sorry. You lost your mother. It's difficult."

Jean-Louis nodded. "I miss her."

Taking his son into his arms, Rez hugged him. And when he thought to pull away, instead he pressed him closer. They had never been a demonstrative family. That was stupid. A man should hug his son more often. Because it was only he and Jean-Louis now. They must be there for one another. And he'd not been attentive enough over the past few years.

"I should have done better," he said over his son's shoulder. "Talked to you. Been there for you when you were grieving for your mother. I'm sorry."

When he pulled away, his son's eyes were watering with tears. He nodded. So much like his father. Staunch. Proud. Always there to do what had to be done. He'd taken the reins of Le Beau while Rez had been recuperating. He'd proved himself at a time when he should have been allowed to step back and grieve. *He does have what it takes.*

"She lives in this house," Jean-Louis said. "Her memory…"

Rez winced and stepped back. There was no easy way to breach the next topic. "I must let you know that I've decided to put the mansion up for sale."

"What?"

"Jean-Louis, it's for the best."

"What best? Papa, I just told you how much this

place means to me. I come here sometimes. Just to…to sit in the garden. To remember her."

And Rez had had the audacity to think his son retreated here to escape his wife. That their marriage was in trouble. He really had been more disconnected from his son than he'd realized.

"And Grandmère uses it."

"I… I need to do this, son."

But *did* he? He'd not taken Jean-Louis's feelings into consideration during that moment when he'd torn those rose bushes from the ground out of rage over Colette's *liaison*. In that moment he'd not wanted another thing to do with this house. This memory trap.

And yet he'd surfaced from that rage. Viv had been there to help him understand that he could move beyond it—and he was, and he manifested his own anger. If he chose to react differently, then life would proceed differently.

Jean-Louis stood there, one hand propped on the newel post at the bottom of the marble staircase, imploring him with a look on his face that Rez had not seen since his son was a child. A lost look that silently asked, *Why would you say that, Papa? I know what makes me happy. What makes me feel loved.*

"Sorry." Rez splayed a hand before him. "I wasn't taking you and Coral using the place into consideration." Perhaps there was a way they could both be happy? "I won't sell the house if you stop badgering me about leaving Le Beau. I will remain CEO of Le Beau. You can do that, *oui*?"

"Papa…" Jean-Louis shook his head. "I will not bargain for my mother's memory."

That had been the wrong thing to suggest. He should have negotiated…given Jean-Louis more responsibility? Yes.

"It's not like that—"

"It feels exactly like that. Listen." Jean-Louis raked his fingers through his hair. A habit of frustration. "I need to be more clear with you. You seem to think that I want to boot you from the company completely."

"Don't you?"

"Of course not! You just need to take some time. You missed an important meeting this morning. You've missed many in the past few years. You need to do some healing, Papa."

"And what about you?"

"I speak of what I know! When I was able to, after your return to Le Beau, I took time away from work. You know that. My wife insists we take a spa every other weekend, and it has been good for me. For my heart. You must do the same. To heal."

"I am! I have. Can't you see? I rarely use the cane now. I work long days and the clients are always beyond satisfied with my work. You know no one creates Le Beau pieces like I do, Jean-Louis."

"You are a master. Le Beau would not be Le Beau without your talent, your designs. I'm talking about healing your head."

"I made an appointment with that doctor you told Penelope to give me the number for."

"You did? Papa, that's…" Jean-Louis bowed his head. He seemed on the verge of tears. Then he nodded and lifted a smile to Rez. "That makes me happy. This doctor is cutting edge. I've researched him. He's top of his field. He's not the stuffy kind that makes you sit on a couch and talk about your childhood."

"I'd do anything for you, *mon fils*. If this will make you happy, I'll go see what this doc has to say. Couch or not."

"I think he can help you. I want to see you happy, Papa. And, *oui*, I know Le Beau makes you happy. I don't want to push you out. I want to assume the CEO position because I think it's time I learned. But, as well, I can take on the paperwork. The office stuff that you now sometimes struggle with. I don't want you to leave. I want you to continue to design and create for Le Beau. I simply want to take some of the load from you. And, really, I won't let any of it happen until you agree to take a vacation."

"A what?"

"Exactly! You don't even know what that word means. Papa, when was the last time you took a break from work that wasn't imposed on you because you were in the hospital? Go to Greece! For a few weeks. Just…take the gardener with you. I saw her supporting you at the ball. She's… good for you."

Rez wanted to shout at his son for suggesting such a thing, and in the next second he wanted to embrace him for his cognizance. "I'm not sure. This is…"

"It's a lot to consider. But, trust me, I'm not trying to be rid of you."

Rez heaved out a sigh. And with that breath his balance faltered. He reached to grasp the newel post, but instead his son grabbed his arm and assisted him as Rez's body went backward. He landed sitting on the step. Now there was no denying he wasn't one hundred percent fit. That he never would be. It was a forever reminder of a horrible day. The day his heart had been broken twice.

"Let me think about this," Rez said.

"Of course. Are you okay?"

He nodded.

"Then I'll leave you to think. Whatever you do, do not list this house until we've talked again."

"I won't. I promise."

Jean-Louis left without another word.

He hadn't made a fuss about Rez's balance issue. It was a kindness that clutched at Rez's heart. He bowed his head into his hands and realized that this was exactly how Viv must have felt when he had handed her the shoe and left her alone. Given her space to come to terms with erratic reality.

Emotions prodded at him to give it all up, surrender, go off and live as a hermit. But Rez shook his head. No, he wasn't a quitter. And he couldn't rightfully wrest this house from under his son's feet as if it was a dirty rug that needed to be tossed out. That would be one more emotional crime against him.

It was time to heal their relationship. And perhaps letting go of some control was the catalyst to that healing.

"Did Jean-Louis leave?" Viv asked softly.

He hadn't heard her approach. Her bare feet were in sight from his bowed-head position. And, if he was seeing correctly, he was pretty sure freckles danced on them just as they did her cheeks and nose.

"He's given me a lot to think about," Rez said.

Viviane sat beside him, tilting her head onto his shoulder. He liked how comfortable she had become with him. He knew he was not making a mistake with her.

"He was angry about me missing the meeting. I told him you were at the emergency room."

"Yes, but I wish you'd told me you had a meeting. I would have been fine on my own."

"I know you would have been. But I made a choice, Viv. And I chose you. I love you. You mean more to me than…"

His work? Had his tattered heart begun to repair? Had it already allowed Viv inside in a way that made him never want her to leave?

"I'm going to pause on the sale right now. I need a few days to think it through."

She clasped his hand. "If that is what you need to do, then I'll support whatever decision you make."

"When will the garden be complete?"

"I need to clean the chandelier. And dig in the English roses that I've purchased to replace the… er…the ones we took out. Then I want to bring in a professional photographer, so I have photos for my portfolio."

"I don't think you'll have any problem making The Plant Whisperer a reality. You do wonderful work, Viv."

"Thank you, but it's snagging the clients that will be the challenge."

"Not if I recommend you to my friends."

"You would do that?"

"Of course. I've seen your work. And I never recommend something that I don't believe is quality."

"How did I get so lucky to meet you?"

"Strangely, it was through my mother-in-law. And I need to call her as well."

"She's reachable?"

"She has been for a few days."

Viv looked up at him with surprise.

He shrugged. "I wasn't going to ruin a good thing."

CHAPTER TWENTY

THE NEXT MORNING Rez kissed Viv goodbye while she lay in bed. He told her he was leaving for work but would be back early for his appointment. He walked out quietly, and she rolled over within the soft sheets to face the Eiffel Tower. What a view. What a man. What a life she could have here in Paris.

Was it even possible?

Certainly, she had started something with Rez. She loved him, and he'd told her he loved her. *"I chose you."* But where would it go from here? Did it have staying power? Was she ready to settle into another long-term relationship?

Yes, she wanted Rez. She wanted Paris. She wanted it all.

But *could* she do this? She did have that prospect in Venice. And after that job Rez had said he'd recommend her to his friends.

How many people could he know with indoor gardens in need of work?

Knowing his financial status, and the set he ran with, probably many. And they were the kind of clientele she sought. If she did a few more jobs, and those clients passed on a good word to *their* friends, this could work.

While her core giddied with the excitement of what might lie before her, that pesky no-nonsense busybody who lived within her said, *Whoa, don't rush ahead. This might be a complete disaster. The Venice job could fall through. The man could break it off.*

And then Viv would be left homeless. In a foreign country.

Broken-hearted.

Closing her eyes, she mentally slashed at the busybody with a sword. Then she wondered what sort of crystal she should stick in her bra that would keep her positive. And then she laughed. She didn't need crystals. She was a strong woman, as Rez had said. She could do this.

Maybe...

All things were worth a try. And she was good at putting in the effort. So it was time to act as if she were already doing it. Time to get to work!

Down in the conservatory, Viv inspected the ceiling. The broken glass pane had been replaced yesterday. The glazier had said the rest of the glass was in good order. Now all that remained was to clean the chandelier and plant the English roses.

As she gathered the cleaning spray and a wash rag, her phone rang. "Kiara! Where are you?"

"Berlin. I got a call from Monsieur Ricard. I'm so bummed."

"Why?"

"He didn't tell you? He's not going to list the mansion. There goes my commission!"

"Oh, I'm so sorry, Kiara. He did tell me, but I'd forgotten about it."

"He said he'd pay me for my time. He certainly didn't have to, but he's already wired a sweet payment into my account. That man is delicious, Viv. Are you going to hold tight to him?"

"As tight as I can."

"Really? Can you make it work?"

"I'd like to. Depends on what he wants."

"Why can't it be what *you* want? If you want the man, tell him!"

Kiara had a point. She was creating a new Viviane Westberg. A worldly, independent, reputable gardening expert. Could that woman get—and keep—her man? When she'd initially arrived in Paris she'd laughed at the idea of snagging a Frenchman. And now...?

"What are you thinking about?" Kiara asked.

"I'm thinking about going for it."

"Yes! Keep me posted."

"I will. So, what's going on in Berlin?"

"It's a stopover. In two days I'm headed to Switzerland. You'll never believe it, but Bowen James is listing his chateau."

"Bowen? Isn't that the guy...?"

"Yes, he's the guy."

"Are you sure this is the right thing to do? Just for a commission, Kiara?"

Her friend sighed. "I want to see him again. I… I owe him an explanation. I mean, I loved him, Viv."

"You did. Well, be careful. And call me if you need anything."

"I will. Oh! I'm sending you the info on that Venetian palazzo. There's been a change in plans from the owner. She's leaving tonight because of a family emergency. Which means you need to fly out immediately to go through everything with her. Can you do that? The flight to Venice is less than a couple hours."

"I can *so* do that. I'll look up flights right now. Send me her address and the details you have. Thank you, Kiara. I owe you so much."

"You owe me nothing. You are the best friend I've ever had. Seeing you happy again is all I need." Kiara kissed the phone. "Love you. Bye!"

Rez clicked off after a call from Jean-Louis. His son's excitement had burst through the conversation. He'd thought about telling his dad in person, but he'd had to call as soon as he and his wife were walking out from the clinic. They were having a baby!

Thrilled at the news, Rez tucked a small jewelry

box in his suit pocket and headed down the hallway at work. He nodded to Penelope.

"I'm going to be a *grandpère*. Exciting, *oui*?"

"Yes! I'm so happy for Jean-Louis and his wife. And you! Are you leaving for lunch?"

"I have some things to take care of this afternoon. I don't have anything on my schedule." *Except an appointment with the shrink.* He paused, holding the door handle. "Penelope, do you think Jean-Louis would make a good CEO of Le Beau?"

Her answer was immediate. "I know he would. He's smart, quick to learn, and he knows the business. Just like his dad."

"You're on Team Jean-Louis, Penelope."

"I'm on Team Ricard. I know you feel like Jean-Louis taking your place would be pushing you out. But, Monsieur Ricard, it would be like having two great minds at the top. You'd have less paperwork. Which you know you hate. And you'd have more time to design."

"I'm still going to get you a shirt that says *Team Jean-Louis*." He winked at her. "*Bonjour*, Penelope. See you tomorrow morning."

News of a grandchild made him float. By the time Rez stood before the mansion door he realized he'd walked the whole way from the office. And he hadn't once felt pain in his leg. This was what happiness felt like.

But when he opened the door his mood dropped. Viviane stood in the foyer. With a suitcase.

Rez's heart took a dive. Suddenly his leg hurt like hell.

"Oh, Rez! I wasn't sure I'd see you before leaving."

"Where are you going?"

"Venice. I told you about the job there."

"But you're not finished here."

And she'd agreed to go with him to the doctor this afternoon. It had taken every ounce of his pride to ask her to accompany him. He couldn't fathom doing it alone.

"I just talked to Kiara. The seller of the Venice place needs to see me this afternoon, before she leaves. This will be my only chance to win the job."

"Were you intending to simply leave if I hadn't come home?"

"Oh, Rez, this is a quick trip. One day in and then out. I'm told the flight is only two hours."

"But you've packed all your things?"

She gripped the suitcase handle. "Yes. I…uh… You've gone above and beyond with your kindness in letting me stay here. And the job is almost complete, so I figured… Well… I didn't want to push."

Rez wanted to shout *Push!* But he couldn't find the word. He couldn't speak. She was leaving. As if he didn't matter to her.

"My flight leaves at two, so I'll have to get to the airport soon. I need to call a cab."

"No, Henri will drive you. He'll have you there in half an hour. Viv."

He swallowed. What to say? She was following her dream, and it was leading her to Venice. The woman was independent and smart, and she knew what she was doing. He couldn't stand in her way. He might never be able to give her what she needed. He could financially, but she would never accept that. It was a guilt-free, open heart that Viv required from him.

He pressed a palm over his heart. The square box in his pocket reminded him. Damn it, he'd wanted this to be a special gift. One he'd give to her and then…

And then what? He couldn't ask her now. Could he?

"Will you call Henri?" she asked. "I would love to take you up on the offer."

"Of course." Rez texted Henri. The driver replied that he'd be out front in ten minutes. "So, you're leaving?"

"Please don't give me that puppy dog face. I'll be back late tonight. Or maybe tomorrow morning. I'll just have to see how long it takes. Then I'll finish the conservatory. Promise. Look at me! Jet-setting across Europe to build my business."

The last thing he wanted to do was deflate her excitement.

"I'm proud of you. And I hope you'll return." *To me.* "I can go to the doctor by myself."

"Huh?" She started walking toward the door. "Oh, no, Rez, I completely forgot! The appointment with the psychiatrist." She dropped the suitcase handle. "That's tomorrow afternoon, surely?"

He shook his head. "This afternoon. Don't worry about it. I can do it on my own." He puffed up his chest. It didn't feel right, but he wouldn't show her that she'd let him down. "This is important to you. And, like you said, Venice is a quick trip. I'll see you soon, *oui*?"

The woman he loved was walking away from him. She'd packed her bags, already prepared for the next job. Rez wanted to throw himself in front of her and tell her to stay. They had begun something. One day away from her would feel like forever. Could they survive a long-distance relationship?

"Oh, I can't go. I promised you."

"I insist you go to Venice, Viv. This is your dream job. I can see the doctor by myself. I am a big boy."

"You are. But…" She sighed. "Are you sure?"

No. "Of course I am. Now, go. Henri is always early."

She kissed him quickly. Too quickly. "I'll call you as soon as I get back. Okay?"

"Of course."

As she walked toward the parked limo, Rez whispered, "Come back to me."

And his heart, which had recently begun to stitch itself back together, fissured again.

That had been the single cruelest thing she had ever done to a man. Leaving him standing in an open doorway. Dashing off without so much as an *I love you*. And she had forgotten about her promise to accompany him to the doctor.

Oh, Viv, what a terrible person you are!

She considered telling Henri to turn around. But Venice, and her future, pleaded for her to continue forward. Could their new love survive long distance? She hoped so. This was going to be a test.

A test in which Rez had already answered one question incorrectly. Standing there with her packed bags, she'd hoped he might suggest she stay with him at the penthouse when she returned to Paris. He hadn't. So that meant he wasn't prepared to make that offer to her.

Would he ever?

If he wasn't ready to commit, she had to be prepared to move forward with her original plan. Build her business. Travel the world. Live out of a suitcase from job to job. She could do that. But her heart screamed that it had found a place—a person—it wanted to be close to. Always.

Once at the airport, Viv headed to the ticket counter and waited in line.

Despite the lack of invitation to stay at the penthouse, the disappointment in Rez's eyes when she'd dismissed him for her own needs tugged at her heart. This Venice job was important. But was it more important than keeping a promise to the man with whom she had fallen in love?

The line moved forward ahead of her.

Viv turned and scanned through the window where cabs were dropping people off for departure.

'I chose you.'

He had chosen her over his work. That meant something.

And now it was her turn to make a choice.

After a long shower, Rez sat on the edge of the bed with a towel wrapped about his hips. The doctor's appointment was in an hour. He glanced at his phone. Viv hadn't called. She was probably on the plane right now. It was good that she'd gotten the job offer. She needed to go and confirm that job. He wouldn't stand in her way.

But that meant he had to go to the doctor by himself. He'd spent days, weeks, months going to doctors following the accident. Always by himself. Nervous. Unsure. It had put him out of his comfort zone, and that loss of control had messed with him. Sometimes he'd glance to his side to see if he might find Colette sitting there. Someone, *anyone* to support him while he navigated the cruel and confusing world of the medical system.

"It's why you need control," he muttered aloud.

Realizing that hurt his heart. A heart that had been tattered, damaged, and torn apart over the past years. A heart he could not fix by standing firm at Le Beau. Being CEO meant nothing to him if his heart wasn't whole.

Viv had made him feel as though he could be whole.

And now he was alone again.

Once dressed, he headed down to the foyer. Henri waited outside. Limping to the door, Rez looked at the cane sitting in the umbrella stand.

"Hell."

He grabbed the cane and hobbled outside to the waiting limo. Opening the door, he slid into the back seat and—

"Viv?"

She plunged into his arms and kissed him. "You're not going to the doctor alone."

"But— No, I can't allow you to ruin your chance with the job— Are you sure?"

"I've never been more sure of something in my life. I'll catch the next flight out, after you've been to the doc. I may catch the owner in time—I may not. But to imagine you sitting with the doctor by yourself...? If there's one thing I learned in those years of accompanying my husband to the oncologist it's that patients need advocates.

Someone to sit beside them and listen. Because you may think you hear it all, but you're going to be in patient mode—nervous and anxious. I'll be there to take notes and make sure all your questions get answered. Deal?"

"I love you."

He kissed her, and she pulled him into the deepest most comforting hug he had ever gotten.

The moment the visit was finished, Rez grabbed Viv's hand and rushed her outside to the waiting limo. *Sans* cane! He guided her into the back seat and told Henri to race to the airport. They arrived twenty minutes before the four o'clock flight was due to leave.

She kissed him quickly and promised to be back in the morning.

He couldn't imagine spending a night alone without her snuggled against his body. He waved as she raced inside the airport and Henri pulled away from the curb.

The doctor's visit had been unique and interesting, and he had actually walked out of the office with hope. The doctor, who was indeed a psychiatrist, had initially put Rez through a brain scan. He'd then gone over those digital scans with Rez and Viv. Viv had not let go of his hand. And she had asked some important questions he'd not even considered. Her strength had become his own.

According to the doctor, there were some

things Rez could do to actually mend his damaged brain. The first things, among many, were nutrition and meditation! He'd been sent home with a protocol to follow for the next three months before he would return for another scan to see if improvements had been made.

If the things the doctor had suggested could create clearer thinking and defeat the dizzy spells Rez was on board. And Viv had been excited to help him.

Now he hoped she would be in his life long enough to see him improve.

CHAPTER TWENTY-ONE

DURING THE RIDE from Charles de Gaulle, Viviane watched the red taillights buzz by. Henri had been waiting curbside to pick her up. Even though it was close to midnight. She appreciated the darkness, because she had been tearful since leaving Italy.

Viv had landed at the Venetian airport around six p.m. It had taken her too long to navigate the Italian signage and finally hail a cab to the dock, where Rez had reserved a water taxi for her. She'd frantically knocked on the seller's house just as the front door had opened. The homeowner, a gorgeous woman in her eighties, with silver hair and stunning fashion sense, had frowned at her.

Viv had been late and the owner had had to catch her own water taxi. There had been no time to show her the garden. And really…? Had Viv actually expected to be hired after showing up so late?

Viv had apologized and thought about explaining, but she knew better. It had been her choice to stay with Rez and accompany him to the doctor. She'd known there was a chance she might lose the job.

What really made her feel awful was that Kiara had done this for her as a favor, and she had blown it. She'd texted Kiara with apologies before flying back to Paris. Kiara still hadn't replied.

Blowing out a shivering breath, Viv settled against the seat. It had been a long day. Beginning with the excitement over the chance of nabbing another job, then the struggle about whether or not to actually leave Rez behind to visit the doctor on his own. The decision to go with him had felt so right as she'd sat there, holding Rez's hand, listening to the doctor's hopeful diagnosis. Then had come the rush to the airport and the disaster in Venice. She'd cried silently most of the flight back to Paris. Because she'd failed.

Before leaving Venice, she had texted Rez about her loss. She'd told him she wanted to spend the night in a hotel. That distance felt necessary. Crying in front of him was not what a strong, smart woman would do. Although she hadn't confessed that in the text.

He'd texted back telling her not to worry and that he'd send Henri to pick her up. A hotel room would be waiting for her. His kindness had spurred the tears again. Yet to think of not seeing him tonight brought on even more tears.

Would she get any job now? Sure, it had been only this one job she'd lost. And Rez had offered to help. But who was she to think she could grow an international gardening business without clients or any sort of visibility? She was just an American woman who had jumped into a fantasy. No one in Europe knew about her silly book or the experience she had. No one was going to be excited to hire her. She was a nobody. One amongst many, surely, who might already have a corner on the indoor garden business.

"What have I done?"

More tears flowed as she circulated through the same thoughts over and over. What a fool she had been…

She tugged out her phone and contemplated texting Rez. She knew he would do anything for her. But it didn't feel right asking for what she really needed. A hug. A kiss to make it all better. And really the French lover was all a fantasy, too. It wasn't meant to be. It couldn't be. Not without any means to support herself so she could remain in Paris and be near that lover.

Time to return to Minnesota and lick her wounds.

But she couldn't do that until she'd finished what she'd started. There were minor fix-ups and some staging to do in the mansion's garden. And photos to be taken.

"Henri, take me to the mansion," she said.

Tucking her phone back in her purse, she closed her eyes and cried more silent tears until Henri announced they had arrived at the mansion.

Walking into the cool, dark foyer, Viviane dropped her suitcase by the door. Moonlight beamed in, forming a direct line to the conservatory. She stepped out of her shoes and padded into the garden.

Inhaling the fresh verdancy overwhelmed her.

Rushing to the sofa, Viv landed on it as tears spilled down her cheeks.

Rez quietly strode toward the conservatory. Henri had called him from the limo, informing him of Viv's changed plans. Rez had considered allowing her the peace to simply be alone tonight. But despite her wanting him to believe she needed to be away from the mansion to get out of his way, he couldn't let it end like that. He had been waiting in the hotel room for her. To simply be there for her.

The American woman's style of wearing her heart on her sleeve and asking tough questions, barging in where most dared not emotionally tread, had worn off on him.

Smiling to think how she had changed him, he wandered into the conservatory. She was sitting on the sofa, sniffling. When he got close, she startled and looked to him.

"Rez? I said I wanted to be alone tonight."

"I know what you said. But you really don't want to be alone."

She swallowed back tears, but couldn't stop a few from rolling down her cheeks. "I don't. But… How did you know…? Henri?"

"He looks out for me. And obviously you. I was waiting at the hotel for you."

"You were?"

"I didn't think you really wanted to be alone. But I don't understand why you returned here if you had intended to stay away?"

"I've been a bit scattered lately. Sorry. But I have to finish this project. I just need to pull myself together and— There's sweeping and polishing, and I need to check the new roses—"

"That can wait until morning. I understand why you came looking for me at my penthouse. Because you couldn't stay away from me."

She wobbled her head and admitted, "Yes."

"I know that, because that's how I feel now. I cannot dream of letting you handle this alone. I love you, Viv. I want to be here for you."

She exhaled. "The job…"

"There will be other jobs."

She shook her head. "I doubt it. I'm a failure! But I guess I got what I deserved after I was so mean to you."

"Mean?" He sat beside her and pulled her against him. He brushed aside the hair from her forehead.

"Yes, mean. I left you to go to the doctor all alone," she said.

"But you came back for me."

"Sure, but only after I got hit with guilt at the airport. I had to return. I love you."

He tilted his forehead to hers. Her gaze glinted in the light from the chandelier. "And I had to be here for you. I love you."

With nothing more to say, Viviane melted against him. His arms wrapped about her, stealing away worry and disappointment.

They understood one another.

His hand sliding up her back, Rez held on to the one thing that meant the world to him. Yes, even more than Le Beau. Because he couldn't be happy creating diamond necklaces for other women if he did not have the love and support of this woman. Their mouths met, and he inhaled her want and desire and was goaded deeper into the kiss. Their tongues danced. Their bodies belonged against one another. Supporting without commanding.

"I'm going to have to leave you more often," Viv said when they'd parted. "I felt that one."

"Where did you feel it?"

"Everywhere. If you want to have sex right now, I am so ready." She tugged at his shirt. *Oui?*

"Oui."

Lying entangled with Viv on the sofa, their clothes strewn on the floor and a cashmere blanket flung across them, Rez tilted his head against hers. Her breathing was heavy and deep. He loved it when she orgasmed. She let out a bold, moaning cry every time. No faking for this woman. She was as real and as open as a person could be.

"I love it when you come." He kissed her cheek

and she curled against him, tucking her head against his shoulder.

She laughed. "You give a girl good reason to bellow, let me tell you that. Whew!"

"I want to hear your joy as often as possible."

"I'd like that, too. But…" She sighed, and he felt her mood drop as her body tensed. "When I'm done with your garden, that's it."

"Venice was a letdown, but that doesn't mean you'll never get another job. You shouldn't give up on building a client list."

"I don't want to. I won't. But I don't know how long it will take me to secure another job. Rez, who's going to hire a no-name American woman to create an indoor garden for them when there's probably tons of gardeners who've already staked their claim in Europe? I may have to go home to Minnesota."

"That can't happen, Viv. I love you. I want you in my life. I thought you were intent on the nomadic life? That's what this dream job would entail, *oui*?"

"It does. And will. Oh, Rez, I realize now that it could take some time to establish The Plant Whisperer. But my bank account needs it to happen faster. I really do want to give our relationship a go. But how can we make that happen? I don't think long-distance relationships work."

"Have you ever tried one?"

"No, but…"

"Hell, if you pursuing your dream means I have to boost my frequent flier miles, then so be it."

"You would do that for me?"

"I would."

"Thank you. But, again, my future is uncertain right now."

"I told you I'd recommend you to my friends."

"Sure, and I'd love that. But how many friends do you know who have indoor gardens that actually need work? They probably already have a regular gardener."

He shrugged. "I'll make some calls today. And if you need to stay in Paris a while, you can stay at the penthouse with me."

"That doesn't sound like a long-term invite."

"It can be."

"Rez." She sat up, pressing a palm to his chest. "I do want us to be an 'us,' but I also don't want to rush things. I don't want to force a moving in together situation for either of us. I know you're offering out of kindness, and, yes, you want me in your life, but are you really prepared to have me stay with you? Long term?"

"Honestly? I am. You've made me realize it's time to give up on the guilt. It hasn't gotten me anywhere. Time to move on. For real. And in the process of moving on I have fallen deeply in love with you, and I know it would make me happy to have you by my side all the time. But I also know that if you're working in other locations for weeks at a time it might give us time to ease into the permanent thing. *Oui?*"

"I do like the sound of that. My home base here?"

He nodded. "You've got talent, Viv. Don't sell yourself short. With the right marketing, and word of mouth, your business will grow. Just take it slowly. I will support you. Promise."

"Very well, but there's one more thing. Are you sure you can handle having a relationship with a woman who doesn't even speak your language?"

He chuckled. "*Mon amour*, you will learn."

"I honestly won't. I've tried. French does not stick to my brain cells."

Rez kissed her, rolling her onto her back and crushing his length along hers as he did so. Mmm… He was already hard again. He rocked against her, murmuring something in French.

"Fine," she confessed. "I think I know exactly what you said."

Très bien." He kissed her breasts, then leaned on his elbows. "The language will not be an issue. But I also have one more thing. You should know that I'm turning the reins of Le Beau over to Jean-Louis."

"Really? Are you sure? Le Beau means so much to you."

"Jean-Louis can handle it. He will learn because I will teach him. He's got a plan that'll slowly ease him into the position over the next year. And I won't have as much paperwork or meetings. It's win-win."

"Are you just saying that?"

"No, I mean it."

"Wow. I'm proud of you. And you'll still work there? Get to design beautiful necklaces and rings?"

"I would never walk away from what makes my heart sing."

She kissed him. "I know the change will be right for you. And with the protocol the doctor gave you, things might really start looking up."

"They already have. I have you. And that is what matters most to me. I almost forgot." He grabbed his suit jacket and fished out a small box from the inner pocket. "I finished it."

She opened the box and pulled out a silver chain. On it dangled the moonstone she had purchased, set into filigreed silver. Set above the white stone was a smaller, deep red stone.

"Garnet?"

"Yes. You said moonstone reminded you of Paris."

"Yes, and that garnet was for love."

"Exactly. But also the garnet reminds me of you, Viv. Earthy, sensual, and sexy. I hope you don't mind that I added it."

"Not at all. This is so much more pretty than I imagined it could be. Put it on me."

He secured the necklace behind her neck and the weight of it landed above her breasts. Viviane pressed a palm over it.

Rez leaned down and kissed her cheek. "This means there is someone in Paris who loves you. Who wants you to move in with him. Let's have fun with one another. Let's be lovers. Have sex whenever we want to. Eat at all hours of the day. Dash off to exotic locations. Jean-Louis wants me to take a vacation."

"How do you feel about that?"

He shrugged. "More good than bad. But relinquishing control over Le Beau will be a scary adventure for me, much as your future will be for you."

"We'll be there for one another."

"Deal. Do you want to go to Greece for a few weeks and forget about the world and have sex all the time?"

"Yes," Viv said without thought.

Because she didn't need to think about it. She was diving in deep with this man.

And life had never felt more promising.

EPILOGUE

A week later...

VIV'S PHONE RANG but she ignored it. The water was as impossibly blue as Rez's eyes. They sat on a private beach on a Greek island, sipping retsina, making love, and talking about anything and everything except their jobs.

Rez nudged her and handed her the phone. "It's an American number. You should take it."

Reluctantly, she did, wiping the sand from the phone while Rez began to kiss down her bare stomach. She whispered, "Wait until after this call before doing that."

With a groan, he rolled over and shaded his eyes from the sun with a hand.

Viv answered the call. It was Evangeline, the woman she'd spoken to at the Le Beau *soirée*. She and Nestor had moved into their Sixteenth Arrondissement home and were desperate for the terrace garden to be put in order. As well, they wanted her to teach them how to care for the plants. Was she available?

She glanced to Rez and their eyes met. His expression brightened as he seemed to hook onto the giddy feeling that was dancing through her system. He leaned over to kiss her on the head.

"I am," she finally said. To Rez—and their future—but also to her prospective client.

She heard the woman shout enthusiastically and tell someone The Plant Whisperer would do it.

The Plant Whisperer had done it.

Viviane had taken a leap into a new and wonderful future. And there was no looking back now.

* * * * *

*If you're curious about Kiara Kirk's
story look for*
The CEO and the Single Dad
coming soon!

AUTHOR NOTE

IN REGARD TO Rez's traumatic brain injury, during my research I discovered a doctor who'd created a unique approach, not just inviting the patient to sit on a couch and talk about his issues, but rather to scan the brain and see what was really going on inside his damaged brain.

I did not want to detail too much in the story. Every patient is different, and I am not a doctor. Nor would I ever suggest what the best treatment might be for any particular individual. But if you're interested check out the psychiatrist Daniel Amen for more information on his breakthrough therapy.